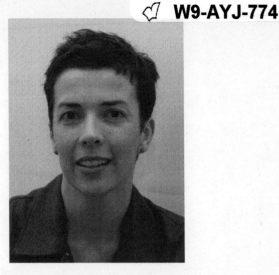

Lara Fergus grew up in the western suburbs of Sydney and gave up a science degree to become a contemporary dancer. Some years and an ankle injury later she gave that up to see the world and wash dishes. She spent seven years living overseas, mostly in France. In that time she completed degrees in writing, women's studies and international law, and worked with various advocacy organisations, including for newly arrived immigrant and refugee women.

She has now worked as a researcher and writer on human rights—particularly violence against women—for over a decade, with organisations such as Amnesty International, White Ribbon, VicHealth and most recently the United Nations. She currently works for the Victorian Government on policy to prevent violence against women. She lives in Melbourne with her partner Maryse, writes before work and dances on the weekends. *My Sister Chaos* is her first novel.

Lara Fergus

MY SISTER CHAOS

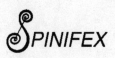

Published in Australia by Spinifex Press in 2010

Spinifex Press Pty Ltd
504 Queensberry St
North Melbourne, Victoria 3051
Australia
women@spinifexpress.com.au
www.spinifexpress.com.au

Cover image by Suzanne Bellamy, http://www.suzannebellamy.com/
Cover design: Deb Snibson, MAPG
Printed by McPherson's Printing Group

For permission to reproduce image on p. 147, thanks to Dan Wills for the Nova Fractal http://ultraiterator.blogspot.com/

National Library of Australia
Cataloguing-in-Publication

Fergus, Lara.
My sister chaos / Lara Fergus.

  ISBN 9781876756840 (pbk.)
  ISBN 9781742195025 (ebook: DX reader)

  Sisters—Fiction.

A823.4

Contents

For my sister Monica
and our mothers

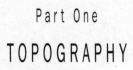

Part One

TOPOGRAPHY

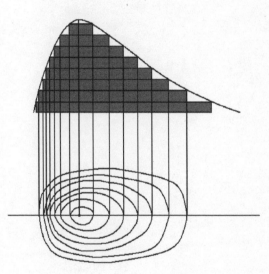

Chapter 1

The house is lit up when I arrive home. I can see that nothing has been disturbed. There are no footprints but mine on the path; through the window next to the door I can see everything is in its place. The clear surfaces, the swept fireplace, the maps tucked in their row of folders. The usual. First the security door, then the inner door. Once inside, the chain and bolt. I pad through the rooms, flicking off the lights. The hum of the bulbs is silenced, the blue of the evening seeps through the blinds. In the kitchen I gulp a glass of water where I stand, my lower back pressed to the sink. Wash the glass, dry it, replace it. The twilight cool in my mouth.

I see well in the dark, at least better than others, which is all that counts. And I know the layout of the house, the furniture, what to avoid, where I could hide. This is my advantage, should I need one. I allow no distractions: no television, no radio, no armchairs or couch. Just shelves around the walls and the great sloping draftboard in the centre. The most beautiful thing I own, the first thing I bought on arrival, as soon as I could afford it. Some of the others won't buy anything they can't carry or fit in a car boot. But I will not move again. I have to take up some space after all.

I close the blinds, and feel for the edge of the draftboard in the dark. It's set at its minimum height, but the slope starts at my lower ribs: they don't make these things for small women. I find the texture of the paper with my fingertips. Smooth it to its edges with the flat of my palms, the full length of my arms. I strain my eyes to make out last night's markings. Good exercise for the rods in the retinal layers, but the finer detail is, as always, impossible to decipher without more light. I reach under the draftboard and unhook the lamp I sewed into a headband at the camp. It is portable and convenient, though I'm aware it makes me an easy target. There are some necessary risks. I slide it down to grip my forehead and turn it on. The map lights up like a revelation.

The usual. Awe, briefly. Two or three seconds where I am stunned by the perfect angles, the precision of line, the telescoping detail into which the eye falls and falls. I straighten my back. Pride, almost. Then the lacunae, like watermarks, seeping up through the grain. There's so much more work to do.

I am crouched at the front door, measuring its distance from the adjacent wall, when the unexpected happens. The crunch of gravel on the path outside. I keep my head bowed, reach to my forehead, squeeze off the headlamp. Darkness, and the sound of bats squabbling in a neighbour's tree. I straighten up with my arms held out from my body to avoid rustling my clothes. The crunching has stopped on the other side of the door. I keep my feet planted and twist my body to the peephole. A vague profile lit from the street. My sister. She raises her fist and knocks: loud and arhythmical.

She will spoil everything. The carelessness of her movements, the heat of her arms, the eddying of air in her wake. I can't let her in. I would have to redo all the measurements so far.

—I know you're there because the lights are off.

She speaks in our mother tongue, which I've barely heard for two years. As if the door were no barrier, and she were

4

playing one of our childhood games—the one where she'd stretch a hand over her eyes and point to where I was in the room. I know you're there because the floorboards creaked, she'd say. I know you're there because you make a shadow. My ear pressed to the door now I can hear her breathing. Then she says she can hear mine. It's no use.

—Who's dead? I ask.

—No one, open the door.

Face to face she is tall and formless in her baggy clothes.

—Money? I ask.

—No.

The last time I'd seen her we were in 'temporary accommodation': a cardboard motel on the city's outskirts. She buzzed with irritation, loathed everything about this new place, railed against the apathy of its people, the ugliness of its architecture, the inefficiency of its public transport. She would not stay. When the settlement adviser came, she accepted his leaflets politely, like me—language courses, medical assistance, housing services—then shoved them in the bin as he closed the door behind him. She would not settle into exile, she said, would not make exile a daily routine. The next day she was gone. She was the last person I had to learn to live without.

—Are we going to stand in the doorway all night? she asks.

I step aside. She's carrying a backpack, so stuffed full she can only squeeze forward. I bolt the door behind her. She flicks on the overhead light, drops the bag to the floor and looks around. It must look bare. Perhaps she wants an armchair to flop into, or, it occurs to me, something soft to sleep on. She sees me eyeing the backpack.

—There's something in it for you, she says.

—What?

She unzips the top pocket and takes out a small parcel.

—This. Happy birthday.

—It's today? I say.

—Of course it's today.

—I didn't get you anything.

She laughs.

—That's the advantage, you see, of being a twin, she says.
—There'll always be someone who'll remember your birthday.

—Sorry.

—Doesn't matter, she says. —You didn't know I'd be here.
Open it.

—What is it?

—A bowl. I made it myself. Do you like it?

An irregular mass of clay and glaze, barely convex.

—I don't think it'll sit properly, I say.

—It sits. Look. Now you've got something on your mantelpiece.

—What's it for?

—You know. Knick-knacks.

—Knick-knacks?

She shrugs.

—Yes.

I make her coffee. We stand and drink it, me in the kitchen,
her blocking the doorway. She waves her hands as she speaks,
the coffee mounting the side of her cup, spilling over the edge,
slopping onto the floor. She pulls a tissue from her pocket,
drops it and pushes it over the linoleum with her boot to soak
up the liquid. She says she wants to stay, for 'a while'. I offer
money for a hotel room, but she refuses. She'll be no trouble,

she insists, and has enough food and everything else she needs. She can sleep on the floor, no problem, she says.

If I think of her as someone I just met she'd be almost bearable. I'd probably like her, in the casual way she moves, the sense of humour in her eyes. She wouldn't be someone I'd make an effort to get to know better, but then again no one is. It's the association I can't stand, the fact that she's related to me, the way she drags me back.

I tell her I'm working here, but that confuses her—she has assumed, rightly, that I would be employed by now, somewhere professional, where my work would be external. I explain that it's a personal project.

—Since when is cartography personal? Isn't it a fieldwork thing?

—Depends. But I need quiet, and space.

—Depends on what?

—On what you're mapping. So you can't stay. I'm sorry.

She goes. From behind the door I hear her steps retreating on the gravel path. I turn off the lights. Hear the creak of the gate as she shuts it behind her. I've lost less than an hour.

The problem with my work is level of detail. Knowing where to stop. Do I take contours every metre, every centimetre, every millimetre? I'm trying every two centimetres now, but that small dent in the floorboards, for instance—made by the men who delivered the draftboard—is not represented; it falls between the measurements. But if I make the scale larger I have to restrict the space being mapped, which is another misrepresentation. I have to choose between detail and scope, both of which are, ultimately, limited. Even if I choose a large scale —more detail, less scope, smaller area—to try to achieve something approaching accuracy, there is always something missed. All maps are lies. So far, that is.

The next morning on my way out I find my sister curled like a snail outside the gate. As I close it behind me she opens her eyes. She looks soft, exposed.

—This is emotional blackmail.

—No it's not, she says. —I have to sleep somewhere.

—If you're going to sleep outside you could sleep anywhere. But you chose to sleep in front of my house.

—Well I don't know this city. But you wouldn't live any-where dangerous.

—Everywhere is dangerous.

—I'm not talking about war. I'm talking about muggings, rape, murder, that sort of thing.

It is emotional blackmail.

—I'm going to work, I say.

I have sometimes thought of her, over these past two years. When I have been tired, or doing a mundane part of the map. I see her as a child in our living room back home, small in the armchair, legs swinging. Her fingers rummaging through our mother's cosmetics case she has taken from the bathroom. She finds a shell pink bottle which she opens to reveal a tiny brush attached to the lid. I go close to her to see the bottle, smell its unfamiliar paint-like fumes, I am close to her and so small myself that I have to look up to see her face. She takes my hand and paints my nails.

Allowing myself to think of her like this seems a weakness, and is something I regret afterwards. Like indulging a craving for some sweet, nutritionless food.

My current task at work is relatively straightforward: mapping the contracting borders of island states as sea levels rise. I need only follow procedure, which is largely a matter of setting the correct algorithms and the computer does the rest. In my position before the war I would have delegated such a simple task to an intern. But we have to accept these demotions. I am lucky to have a job in my field—not many of us do. I am lucky, indeed, to be alive. Or so I am repeatedly told.

As the computer deals with the figures I watch the shores change shape, obliterating the coastal towns, flooding over peninsulas, eliminating previously safe harbours. The usual. All the elevations have to change, which is the most disruptive part of the process. Sea level has always been the constant, the zero. But the computer copes with that too.

I can do all this without thinking, and concentrate instead on the methodology of my personal project. If I map canonically perhaps it can be done. A repetition of phrase in different scales. I need to start broad, then add detail in smaller measures. Length and breadth from the walls for structure, depth from the minutiae of texture, resonance from the accuracy of the whole.

Chapter 2

When I arrive home the house is lit up. All is as I left it, including my sister crumpled at the gate. What's changed is her mood, she's now tired and cranky. She asks me what's wrong, why I hate her so much, what she could possibly have done. I don't hate her at all, though, and she's done nothing, nothing I can hold her to anyway. She just doesn't understand that I have to work.

—Why can't you work with me in the house?

—Because you'll change it.

—Change what?

—The house. What are you doing here anyway? You decided to leave and you left. Why do you want to stay here now?

—Because I've got some things I want to do. Some of my own work, okay? For god's sake, I'm your sister, I'm passing through town and I want to sleep on your floor for a few days. It's not unheard of.

She is not yet at the end of her tether. I would recognise it if she were. She could sleep outside for days, but the neighbours would call the police eventually. I know these police are not like our police, that I should have nothing to fear if they knock at my door. My ethnicity is not evidence here; I could tell them that I am not responsible for my sister, that her actions cannot condemn me. But I would be questioned, and though I've committed no crime, would have to lie. Out of habit, and out of the knowledge that my behaviour would seem unreason-

10

able to an independent observer. I know that, I'm not mad.

Once inside she opens her backpack and extracts a plastic bag filled with dirt-covered vegetables. —I'll cook you dinner, she says. She goes to the kitchen and starts washing, peeling, slicing. The skins of things dropping to the floor, squashed and smeared under her boots. From the map room I catch glimpses of her muddy hands sliding over the taps, the bench, the chopping board.

I grip the corners of the draftboard, breathe through my nose and try to concentrate, but it is impossible to calculate anything with the incalculable happening only metres away. The smell of the spices she's using pulling me backwards into the past, into the orange Formica kitchen of the house where we grew up. The plywood cupboards plastered with a layer of dark brown wood, the edges full of grime which bothered me more than my sister and bothered my mother most of all. How she would rub at them with a wet teacloth while the saucepan overflowed behind her.

I keep my eyes on the map, willing its intricacies to curl around my mind and draw me in, to the calm, mathematical order of its lines. But the clatter of plates keeps it all at a distance, then her voice, too loud for the smallness of the space, asking, —Where do you eat?

I look up. She's holding open the kitchen door with her elbow, two plates steaming in her hands.

—In the kitchen, I say.

—There's no table.

—There's the bench.

I take a plate from her hand and wait for her to step back so that I can pass. The kitchen is all disorder—like a bomb has

11

hit it, as they say here. I eat with my plate on the bench, looking neither right nor left. She's cooked a dish from home. Not one I ever particularly liked. In any case you can't get all the ingredients here. She holds her plate in one hand, a fork in the other. I glance up and sense her disappointment with the whole situation. She puts her plate on the bench to take up a glass of wine.

—This is homely, isn't it? she asks.

She's being sarcastic of course. But I realise that's what she wants. Home. Though perhaps not the place she was born and grew up in. She is homesick for a place that doesn't exist any more, the sort of place that would welcome her, and that she would want to live in. Did she really expect to find it here?

I don't do nostalgia. I can barely remember what life was like before the war. I don't mean that the war seemed long, on the contrary. It mounted with unnerving speed, and broke upon us before we realised what it was. Our lives were washed away in a matter of weeks. But my memory of the time before it is smudged. My homeland, what I did there, where I went to work or ate my lunch, who I spoke to, who I knew. It all seems far away, like childhood. Was I happy? Did I feel safe? All I can remember is that I used to make maps like painting, with the joy that comes from representing something on paper, symbolically, for the sake of it, for pleasure. Now it is a necessity. There is far too much inaccurate mapping out there these days. You can talk about perception and the ambiguity of truth, but my instruments are accurate and ten centimetres is ten centimetres no matter who's looking at it. I might not trust newspapers, or photos, or speeches, but I should be able to trust maps.

When I packed, I left behind photos, letters, anything that would weigh me down. Everything except daily necessities, and a single USB memory stick. Memory in its most unsentimental form, memory as data, a memory more complex than the human brain could hold. The only memory I want to keep.

Chapter 3

The house is lit up under my hands as I work, my instruments glinting in the glow of my headlamp. The drafting paper swells in front of the sliding ruler as I draw it down the slope to align once more with this back wall which has been giving me so much trouble. I hear a noise and look up to see my sister in the doorway. She has finished the dishes and now flicks off the kitchen light behind her. I track her with the headlamp as she feels her way through the dark of the map room to the opposite corner.

She leans back into the angle of the two walls and slides down to sit on the floor, stretching her legs out in front of her. With one arm she drags her backpack from where it lies nearby, hauls it to the vertical and props her elbow on top of it, folding her arm up to support her head. She can't possibly see my face behind the headlamp but looks at me as if she can. I can feel the question coming like a migraine. —What are you mapping? she asks.

It's not that I want to keep it a secret, it's just that if I explain it will sound so much less essential than it is. Perhaps that's a good thing, however, the fact that she will not be able to grasp its importance. It could protect me in some way I have not yet conceptualised. So I shrug and say, —I'm starting with the draftboard.

She waits. I swing the headlamp back to the map.

—And then what? she asks.

—And then I'm moving outwards, I say without looking up.

—I see.

—Do you?

—No, she says, —sorry.

I look back at her face. She thinks I've become some sort of recluse who can no longer communicate, so I decide to explain the Point of Beginning. The pinprick made with my dividers at the exact centre of the draftboard, the fixed point from which all other measurements will be made. —The first thing I mapped was the drafting paper itself, I explain. She comes over and I show her how I've pierced the paper at its own centre and held it to the Point of Beginning with a piece of copper wire, tied loosely in place, so I can fit my ruler under the knot.

—The first thing you mapped was the map? she asks.

—Yes and no. Yes the paper that the map's now on, but at the time it was just a blank piece of paper, onto which I then drafted a rectangle representing itself. Around the wire—see?

—But you haven't drawn a rectangle within the rectangle?

I breathe in. It's just that when I try to explain it all the problems are exposed, all the contradictions, all the paradoxes, the inevitable errors of all my possible ways.

—I see what you mean, I say, —but no. Because cartography doesn't deal with time. It only deals with what's there when you take the measurements. And when I was taking the measurements of the borders of the drafting paper from the Point of Beginning, there was nothing on the paper. Do you see?

—But that means your map's immediately out of date.

—I know that. All maps are immediately out of date.

—That must be frustrating.

I look at her. I don't know if she's being sympathetic or mocking me.

—You have no idea, I say.

I pick up my ruler to indicate that we have reached the end point of the discussion. She straightens up and walks out of the pool of light made by my headlamp. I watch her out of the corner of my eye, keeping my focus on the map. She slides her hands over the mantelpiece, the shelves, crouches to examine my folders and books. She is looking at everything as if measuring it, but not in the way that I measure things. More like an assessment of shape, an eye to value on some unknown scale. There is nothing neutral about the way she looks.

—Your eyes get used to the dark, don't they? she says.

This is not strictly true but I don't want to risk another conversation by arguing the point.

—Why though, she asks, —do you keep working on something that's already out of date?

I keep my eyes to the draftboard and pretend to measure a line whose length, of course, I already know. She is unaware of the irony of her posing that particular question, and I gauge my response carefully.

—Until recently, I say, —the only thing that was obviously out of date was that one rectangle. Because nothing else in the house had changed.

—Until recently?

—Yes. It is the recent and unexpected addition of new objects which is likely to cause me the most difficulty.

She takes that as personal, which it was. It is also untrue, I realise with some guilt, as the greatest difficulties lie elsewhere.

—Look, she says, —I'm sorry but I don't see the point of it. Are you being paid, at least? By the real estate agent or something?

—Why would they pay me to do this?

—I don't know, maybe the owner wants to sell and they need a floor plan.

—It's not a floor plan, it's a map. What do you think I am? Some sort of trainee designer?

—Oh come on. I mean—you live here, right? Why do you need a map of it?

She says it with the same tone our mother would use when frustrated. As if her failure to understand my actions made them inherently unreasonable.

—Look, I ask her. —How far is it from this wall to the one opposite?

She pauses, wondering if it's a trick question. —I don't know, she says, —three metres?

—Four point two six, and I could go on to five decimal points but I think I've made my point, no pun intended.

—No pun taken. What point?

—That just because you live in a place doesn't mean you know it. That you haven't got the slightest idea. That you've been here for hours and you were out by over a metre.

Chapter 4

When I open my eyes the house is dark. It is the middle of the night and I can hear her breathing, its rhythm matching my own. She is sleeping on the floor, at the foot of my bed. I prefer this to her disrupting my work space. I turn onto my side and through the gloom see her clothes heaped in the corner; nothing folded or stacked. She is entropic, I think, briefly, before sinking back into sleep.

Her sleeping bag rustles through the night, my synapses organising the sound into something that passes for coherence. I dream of leaves, swishing in trees. The fruit trees at her place, before the war. When she is quiet, the leaves fall.

I went out there often, even though it was in such a remote region, not known for its beauty or any points of interest. It seemed normal for us to visit each other back then. She owned the place with several other women, my sister buying in with the little money she inherited when our father died. Some land, and a big building which was once, I think, a sort of barn. It was unrecognisable as such now, with all the extra rooms they built adjacent to, or on top of, or within it. A place full of rooms, most of which I never saw.

And these women. Friendly enough, who would engage you in intimate conversation for short, intense, periods of time and then be gone, back to their own concerns, which were apparently pressing.

I can see them climbing the trees in summer, in sneakers and sun hats, to knock down the fruit. In autumn, the leaves turning, falling, collected in armfuls and thrown into the fire to perfume the air. Some were swept upwards by the heat, becoming small flames dancing past your face. In winter, the flue snaking out of the huge central fireplace would warm the rooms on its twisted path up and out. It must have broken through the roof at a secret point in the top corner of an unknown room, but its smoking exit was unseeable even from the tree tops outside, even from the highest bough.

I looked down from among the branches at dusk, watched them going inside, their curtainless windows lighting up one by one. I felt safe there. In the chaotic swish of the leaves.

My sister turning over in her sleeping bag.

It was all lost, of course, in the war. Land is the worst thing to own. And being tied to a place where you can be found is a dangerous thing. That's why I can't stand the country and I can't stand small towns. I can't stand people looking at me as if I were their business. When I was deciding where to live in this new country, I chose this second-largest city. Not the largest, because that would be too predictable. But big enough. I didn't want to be anywhere uncrowded, anywhere where I was likely to be recognised in public. Some people want that, they think it's important for a community. But they haven't thought it through. You don't really want people caring whether you live or die.

Chapter 5

The house is lit up when I open my eyes. The sunlight angles through the bedroom blinds and stripes the ceiling red-orange above me. My sister is already awake. She sheds the sleeping bag like dry skin and thuds through the corridor to the map room. I hear the zips on her backpack, hard grating sounds on the floor. I am worried that she will move the draftboard, and that would disrupt the project for weeks. My bare feet are cold on the floorboards. From the doorway between the corridor and lounge room I see her sitting on her backpack in the corner, a small wooden structure in front of her. She pulls at it, pushes, finally clicks it into place. An easel. She looks up and smiles. —I made it, she says. Then she squats next to the backpack and rummages for brushes, tubes of paint, a chipped cup, a plastic plate coated in swirls and smudges of dried colour. She pads to the kitchen to fill the cup with water, and returns to settle herself in the corner of the room, sitting on the backpack, to paint.

It's the same backpack she carried when she had finally arrived at my flat, in the city where I used to live, during the war. She was three days later than we'd arranged. By then the fear had got into my bones, I could barely bring myself to open the door. Her friends had dispersed. Perhaps they were captured, she didn't say. Later we heard about the rapes. We left together, me with two suitcases, her with the backpack. At the port there were TV cameras, reporters in their khakis interviewing tearful grandfathers. We passed by unnoticed, thinking about our passports, about which queue we were supposed to join, about whether we should try to buy bottled water, about whether there would be food when we got there, about how we would contact anyone once we arrived, once we left.

On the other side we were shuttled into a camp, in all its disorder, disease, death. She staked out our territory, kept the flaps of the UN-issue tent closed. I sewed my old bike lamp into a headband so we could have both hands free to prepare food. It was winter and there was no electricity: we learnt to live with limited light. After several weeks came the interviews, the paperwork, the confusion about relatives: who was where, who was still alive. Then the endless train and bus trips, tickets handed to us, directions given. Our destination was chosen for us, arbitrarily. We ended up here.

At an internet kiosk in some airport we had set up hotmail accounts, in case we lost each other. I sent her an email the day after she left the motel, left me to remake my life out of nothing but leaflets. No response. I kept sending blank messages, every 89 days, the day before the accounts would deactivate if un-used. After a year I decided to expect nothing more from her. The decision brought me a sense of security, like having walls after a long period in the open.

One day she wrote back, to tell me that an uncle's body had been found in a mass grave. I took this in without analysis. Bit by bit she'd forward fragments of information: so-and-so had been sent to such-and-such a country, someone else was dead. She became a figment of information technology, an email alert, monitoring the movements of relatives and friends through databases: neutral, faceless.

21

Now that she's here the realness of her is disturbing, almost painful.

The house is stuffy despite the coolness of the morning. Her body heat has pushed up the temperature, her breath the humidity. She sits cross-legged and barefoot in the corner, the miniature easel propped up in front of her. She unscrolls a small, half-painted canvas, stretches it and clips it onto the easel frame. It's obvious what she's doing, but I ask anyway. She looks up. I am uncomfortable seeing myself through her eyes and try to relax my body against the doorframe. She doesn't answer my question but goes straight to its intent.

—What is it you disapprove of? she asks.

I suppose I should feel affection for this kind of sisterly insight, but I don't. My arm muscles feel hard against the wood.

—It's messy, I say.

—I haven't finished it yet.

—Not the result, the process. You'll get paint on the floor.

—It'll dry up.

—It'll stain. The liquid components will get into the boards. They'll expand.

She looks at me like I'm mad. I see her examine my face, the way I'm holding my shoulders and hands. —Do you have any newspaper? she asks.

I'm not interested in the politics of this place, even less so in the lifestyle magazines that pass for newspapers here. I don't want to blend in, like some of the others, slough away the past, adopt this new place, or rather attempt to be adopted by it, as an orphan. No place will mother or father me now. Countries are not mine and I am not theirs. I feel nothing for them, they are merely temporary, political intrusions into geographic cartography. There is just me, my draftboard, my rented house. I have what are known as portable skills. Education is where my share of our father's inheritance went, something I could take with me when we had to leave.

I get her a sheet. It's one from home and is too small for the beds here, an idiosyncrasy I hadn't envisaged when packing. She swings the easel under her arm, picks up the cup of water and slides the backpack, brushes and paint tubes out of the way with her right foot. I hand her one end of the sheet, take the other and stretch it out, then lay it on the floor and fold in the two opposite corners along a loose diagonal. My sister follows my lead, helping me tuck under the excess at the sides until we have a right-angled triangle, which I measure as two metres by one point six, by the square root of two squared plus one point six squared. My sister slides the whole triangle into the corner and lifts the backpack on top of it. She is being careful, I can see that. I do my calculations and cut a small triangle of blank paper to scale. I pin it to its corresponding place on my map. For the moment I can ignore that part of the room. I will be able to remove it when she's gone.

I wonder how she's been living. She's learned none of the important languages. She's mentioned washing dishes, cleaning hotel rooms, packing boxes on a production line. She owns only what she left home with—whatever's in the backpack. I don't know how she could know about our relatives before I did. I'd get the official letters months afterwards, if at all, and she had no fixed address. She must be in contact with the relevant organisations, logged onto some internet registry, actively seeking out such information. Why she would do that was beyond me. I suppose she's looking for our mother, who is surely dead.

—Please don't touch anything, I say before leaving for work. It's a meaningless request: she'll unconsciously contact with the walls, the sink, the toilet, the shower and of course the floor. Possibly the kitchen surfaces. My aim is simply to minimise the damage.

—I'll stay here all day, she says from her corner. —Or I could go out if you like. Do you have a spare key?

I measure the alternatives before saying no.

Chapter 6

There had been that surreal, in-between time. It lasted a week or so after the war was officially declared, as the battles intensified in the northern part of what was then our country. The time when we didn't know what it meant, how we should prepare, and for what. So people just continued with their routines: they dropped children at school, caught buses, met friends, did whatever it was that defined and delineated the structure and boundaries of their lives. I went to work.

In my unit we were all working, in some way or another, on the Global Map: an international project aiming to provide data for all land areas on the planet in a standardised form. I say 'my' unit because I was the manager. I was supposed to say 'our' unit, 'our' work, 'our' projects, to encourage a sense of ownership and belonging. But own what? Belong to what? It was about the work, it was about the mapping, and the responsibility to make it happen was mine.

I was considered a little too young for the position, a little too much from the wrong ethnic group, and a lot too female. I made up for it by smiling less and caring more. For the project, that is, for the quality of the work. I pitched my voice low. I set high standards for my staff. I was contained, demanding. I sacked people, I scared people; they would go quiet when I walked into a room. I like to think that people forgot about my age, sex and ethnicity after a while, and grew to hate me for who I actually was. But you can never tell.

I could have delegated project management of the Global Map, but I was drawn to the ambition of it. This single, unified map of everything, or at least everything on the planet above sea level, which was a very good start. I liked the idea of controlling that. So I took it on, organised the collation of existing national geospatial data, the design and implementation of cartographic projects to fill in the gaps, and then the production of a digital dataset for the entire landmass of what was then the country, at a scale of one to one million.

I no longer did any actual mapping. I never left my office except for meetings. I conceptualised it, though, I established the methodology, set the timelines, delegated small sections to different teams. It ran smoothly, it ran to time, people did what they were supposed to do, problems were anticipated and managed.

We were two months off finishing when the war broke out and the borders started collapsing. I told myself it didn't matter. The shifting borders were merely political; an inconvenience from a practical and logistical standpoint, but one which could be dealt with. The landmass itself would remain constant. I would just need to give the relevant data to scientists in the new countries formed by the war, and request data from those in countries which had, literally, lost ground. I readjusted my timelines and began applications for additional funding.

On the day that they told us that they were closing up the building and we had to evacuate I was stunned. I was still working, the project wasn't finished, there was no way I could leave it. In the end someone got a security guard to stand in my office doorway. That was enough. I didn't wait for him to come any closer, my horror of being touched by strangers being stronger than my desire to stay. And I could see that it would seem ridiculous to listeners, when told later, as a story.

But I saved it all. I was the only one who possessed the data in its entirety. The people working for me only had access to the small areas for which they were responsible, and the UN agency that funded the project only got the summarised versions I sent them in reports. I took the data without the programs that would enable me to read it, to save space. It took up surprisingly little memory: a single USB stick which I hung around my neck, tucked into my clothes.

I did it for safety's sake, as a backup, thinking I'd return in a few weeks to continue. I had no sense of heroism, otherwise I would have been more methodical; insisted colleagues save the data on their own projects, made more backups in different forms. We could have emailed the most important files to each other or ourselves. But we were all sure we'd be back, and it was all still there on the server, in the basement. It was still there as I tidied my desk, filed away the documents I had been working on, washed my coffee cup in the office kitchen, the security guard shadowing me. It was all still there as I swiped my way out of the building.

It was all still there until I heard, two days later, exiled in my apartment, that the building had been bombed to rubble. The weight of it collapsing in on the basement and its blinking servers, full of irreplaceable data. Lost, of course. Except what I have, still on the USB stick. My country on a scale of one to one million; my country the way it was before the war anyway. It hangs weightless around my neck.

When I lean forward across my desk here at my new job, I feel it press a cool, metallic rectangle into the skin under the upsweep of my ribs. I pull a print out of a dataset towards me but am finding it hard to concentrate knowing my sister is alone in the house. I am disturbed by the recurring mental image of her getting up and moving off her sheet. She will need to change the water in her cup, it's possible she will knock the draftboard on her way to the kitchen. Worse, the impact might cause her arm to fly up, the dirty water would sweep out of the cup in a brief parabolic arc before splattering down on the map. I should have rolled it up and brought it with me, but there were the pins, holding the triangle in place, and the wire holding the map to the Point of Beginning.

The printout in my hands is a tangle of figures, which I cannot, in this state, decipher. I leave early.

Chapter 7

When I arrive home the house is lit up. I tread beside the path to avoid making noise, out of the sight-line from inside. Gripping the edge of the doorframe, I lean my body sideways until I can see in the window. The usual. The maps are tucked in their folders, the draftboard is undamaged and has not been moved, I can tell by its position relative to the walls. The floor is bare except for the one corner where my sister sits, on the sheet, painting.

It had only been possible because we were together. We worked as a team through the infinitesimally detailed structures of immigration. The sheer weight of practicalities that had needed to be dealt with, the planning, the paperwork—documentary, medical, personal. It was like a puzzle, a game where you didn't know the rules but had to guess them from the actions and reactions of your opponent. We watched the faces of the officials, we made our calculations and adjustments, we told the truth but we made sure we told it in the words that would get us to safety. There were only a few and you had to put them in the right order—we spoke of risk, of persecution, of violence, of torture, of everything we wanted to stop thinking about but couldn't, because they needed the detail, over and over, official by official, with them sitting there, looking just like the soldiers we were describing.

They always think we're lying. The effect of this, on us, is to make the truth seem tenuous. It feels like you might lose it, you start to question your own memories, you start to wonder who you really are. We pushed through the fear. My sister was better at it than I was. She needed my language skills but I needed her bravado, the way she could be sure when I wasn't, the way she stared them down when I flinched. We were a tightrope act, we didn't fall, though many others did, we made it through. We were, in the end, the right sort of refugees.

She looks up and sees me at the window. She flicks her palms upward as if to ask what I'm doing. I pull myself back up to the front door and slide the key into the lock. It's not that I have anything against her. I had nothing to hold her to, after all. No contract, no argument, no recourse. When she left me, in the motel, I searched my suitcase for something to prove my position—that she could not leave me alone in this incomprehensible place. I had nothing. This was a mystery, an oversight that seemed incredible to me, because she did have to stay, and the absence of evidence to support this truth was inconceivable. It was an assumption I had never questioned. It was an assumption she had never held.

Inside it is warmer than usual. I follow my routine, check the rooms, flick off the lights as I go. She doesn't react when I plunge the map room, where she sits, into darkness. As I drink my glass of water I tilt my head around the kitchen doorway. She continues painting in the dark, which shows you how imprecise her process must be. Colours would be impossible to distinguish in this light, let alone line. I rinse the glass, dry it, replace it. Close the cupboard with a click.

Once she was gone I felt as if I had been made less substantial, as if she had evaporated from me. I was honeycombed by her absence. I twisted myself up in the beige motel bedspread wondering if there was anything I could have said or done which would have made it worth staying, made me worth staying for. But I don't think there was. I don't think I had anything to do with it. I think she just had to keep running. Or at least, if she were going to stop, it wouldn't be here.

In the map room I note that everything is in its place except for her triangle of sheet. I scan it with my headlamp. It is already grubby and cluttered with items spilling from her backpack. Plastic bags, newspapers, receipts, books. She has brought in the whole mess of the world. I catch her face in the light. She is looking at me as if waiting for something. I dip the headlamp to the map.

It draws me in. I slide my finest pencil over the contours I have already marked, perfecting their sweep. It is satisfying to have calculated so well that the lines unravel naturally, in simple accord with the principles of representation. There's something about the process of mapping by hand, in this age of computerised cartography. The thickness of the drafting paper, the smell of lead pencils when sharpened. The sensuality of it. And the increased potential for error, of course: the heightened stakes, the way every calculation counts. You need to shut yourself in with your own process like closing doors, the intensity of your concentration muffling all sound from the surrounding world.

I tighten the focus of my high-magnification goggles around the white triangle representing the place where I have put my sister. It's like a scar on the flesh of the map, but one which will peel away in time. She will leave eventually. The objects she has brought permanently into the space, however, will need to be dealt with. I lay my ruler along the mapped cliff-face of the mantelpiece. It is a geometric precipice, rising high above the landscape of the floor, undercut on itself, plunging away with no hope of a slope to slow a fall. And now it is occupied by the bowl my sister gave me. I can sense it there without looking up: a freak of erosion, a free-standing crater. I'll do a sub-map first.

My sister's presence becomes almost ignorable as the evening goes on, consigned as she is to the blanked-out corner of the room. There is just the sensation of heat and movement, the soft swish of charcoal on her sketchpad. Then she says my name. I look up and see her blurred and close through the thick lenses of the goggles. I go to remove them and prick my cheek with my dividers, which I have attached to a wristband for easy access and are now so much a part of my right hand that I forget their sharpness.

—What? I ask. I can just make her out through the goggles—getting up and unclipping something from her easel.

—Do you want to see something funny?

I flick my wrist so that the dividers flip backwards along my forearm, and undo the goggles. My eyes feel sweaty and struggle to focus on the coarse sheet of paper she holds in the light of my headlamp. It's a rough sketch, in black and grey strokes, of a clawed, insect-like figure with bizarre protrusions on its face. Crouched over a draftboard. By the trembling of the paper I know that she is stifling laughter. She tugs the sketch down to reveal her face, composed. —Look at what you have become, she says, in mock seriousness. I smile, as required. I feel a trickle down my jaw. She shoves the sketch horizontal under my chin to catch the drop of blood. It would have landed on the map.

I dab at the puncture in my cheek with a handkerchief.

—Dangerous profession, I joke.

She searches my face for something, something she doesn't find. She gives up and looks down at the draftboard.

—What's this doing here? she says, picking up the bowl.

—Getting mapped.

—You're mapping the bowl?

—Just finished. Look. An above-view contour representation of the bowl, as a mountain, with the rim at zero, or sea level if you like. It's only from the outside at the moment—I'm going to have to do the inside too and then work out how to bring the two together.

She frowns and places the bowl upside down on the map, twisting it to fit the outline. The contour marks disappear.

—Scale one to one, I say, sliding the bowl to one side to expose the map. —Contours every five millimetres.

—Impressive.

—Isn't it? We can see all its irregularities now. Look— every bump, every dent. Even those too small for light to differentiate.

I pick up the bowl and hand it back to her. —It's a sort of improved reality, I say, —don't you think?

As soon as I say that I realise she'll take it personally— again—though this time I didn't intend it as such. —Not 'improved', I begin, but she interrupts.

—You didn't like the reality of the bowl in the first place, she says. —You didn't even think it would sit properly.

I shrug.

—It doesn't, I say.

—It does.

—It doesn't. It rocks.

—It doesn't.

—It does.

—Show me, she says.

—You can't see it. It's not at any level you can perceive—that's my point. The map tells us it must—look.

I point to the warps in the circular contour lines representing the base.

—I don't want to look. What does it matter? Why bother mapping something you already thought was useless in the first place?

I look up at her. Is she blind?

—Illumination, I say. Her expression doesn't change. —Clarification, then. The map illuminates and clarifies the bowl. It heightens the viewer's perception of the bowl in a way that just looking at the bowl never could. Do you see?

—But for what purpose? she says. —I mean, do you even like this bowl?

—What am I supposed to say to that? It was a gift from you and you're asking me if I like it?

—You think it's badly made though?

—Only if you were aiming for symmetry.

—I wasn't.

—So what's the problem?

She picks up the bowl and flips it between her palms. I drop the handkerchief from my cheek. The bleeding has stopped. I hope she'll go back to her painting so I can continue with my work. But she lifts the bowl in front of my face. —Look at it, she says. —See the blue glaze there, how it shines and reflects the light? And the bare clay there?

She shoves it into my hands, takes my fingers and runs them from the rim down to the base of the bowl.

—Feel how the texture changes with the glaze. Take it. Feel how cool it is, the weight of it? That's what I was aiming for, all right?

She pulls the bowl back and places it on the mantelpiece.

—How can you imagine, she says, —that by putting something onto a piece of paper you can improve reality?

The bowl is a good two centimetres off centre. I'll fix it later.

—Going back to your painting? I ask.

She clicks her tongue and looks at me. I try to keep my face as blank as possible.

—Painting's different, she says.

—If you say so.

—I'm not trying to clarify, or even represent, reality.

—Then why do you use real things as models?

—I don't always.

—But you do sometimes.

I hand her back the insect sketch and pull the goggles over my eyes. I'm sick of this conversation. It's like talking to a child.

Chapter 8

The least powerful make the best cartographers. For us it is essential that we know where we are in relation to everyone else. This is not necessary for those who have the power to be at home, for whom the whole world is home. As I step off the tram on my way to work I see a TV through a shop window. Even without sound, I recognise the style of graphics and garish colours. The most powerful of the commercial news networks is showing a map of my country. Cities are marked with small flames to show bombing or sites of conflict. They are all labelled incorrectly. The town I was born in is described by another name. I don't know why this upsets me so much. But it was where I last saw my mother.

I had been home for her birthday, a few months before the war started, more out of duty than anything else. I travelled north to the town from the city where I then lived. As I walked up the hill towards my mother's small house I felt the air thinning, could feel myself becoming smaller, pulling in my boundaries, making myself someone acceptable to my mother and the place she lived in. The town was small, and the predominant colour was grey: grey roads, grey houses, grey sky. The old people were standing, as they often did, in their door-ways; they watched me go by. They knew who I was, where I was going and why. I would have to stop, every couple of houses, come out of my head and into the effort of conversation and expression and memory. I would say hello, exchange pleasantries. Fortunately in the home language you address your elders with an honorific and do not need to use their names, which I had forgotten. They of course used mine.

And then lunch with my mother. Lunch on the rails, the lines we would have to follow, every time we met, to the destination that was the argument. We had a sort of outline for a script within which we improvised: the actual words changed, but the structure was unalterable. It was essentially about shame. Shame, for my mother, that her daughter was not married, that despite, or more likely because of, her education, she had not found a husband, had no children and therefore was not happy. Shame that her daughter had not become a good story to tell the neighbours, a story which could build incrementally as the children grew and she grew old. Shame that her daughter could not then take over and tell the story of her own children to her neighbours, that she had rejected her mother's way of life and perhaps disapproved of it. Shame that now neither of us would ever know what pride was.

My sister had left as a teenager, and never went back there at all. She couldn't, really. The only thing worse than me living alone was her living with other women. We were both more foreign in that town than we ever will be here, in this country of strangers. We shared exile long before the war made it formal.

Chapter 9

The house is lit up when I arrive home. It floats unanchored in the last rays of the afternoon sun. I cross the lawn and curl my fingers between the bricks to hold it down. I have left work early again, my sister's presence making my job seem less important. The conversation of my colleagues today is limited to renovations, shopping centres, football. I can find nothing to say, which makes them think that I don't understand. The irony being that I don't. The irony being that I understand less and less every day.

But I worked hard to gain fluency in this language, even at home before the war. It was essential to keep up with developments in the field, to speak with international colleagues. Since arriving here I have gone further—expanded my vocabulary, perfected syntax, almost eliminated my accent. At interview with prospective employers I knew that if I were to falter in this official language then so too would their perception of my ability in other areas. Even children can conjugate verbs effortlessly in their mother tongue. The inability to do so infantilises the speaker in the eyes of others, in a way that is beyond both logic and justice.

I keep hold of the bricks as I make my way along the façade of the house, my shoes crunching in the crusted garden bed. Through the window I can see that everything is in its place. My sister is in her corner. But something feels different, inconstant. I look down at the window frame, held dry and rough in my hands. The house stills in my grip.

They tell me now I speak too formally for a native, that my perfection of this foreign tongue is what gives me away. My lack of idiomatic phrasing and contractions, my inability to speak casually or clumsily—these things make me suspect. The very thing I believed would help me fit in is now what holds me apart.

I see my sister's hands on the inner window sill opposite mine. I look up: she has come over and stands on the other side of the glass, looking at me from the inside. For a moment I feel stuck to her like a reflection, and can only break away with effort, pulling my retractable tape measure from my pocket and getting back to the task at hand: verification. I extend my arm and hook the metal end of the tape to the right corner of the house between the eighth and ninth rows of bricks. This is level with the Point of Beginning inside. I edge backwards away from my sister, stretching the tape taut across the house's façade to the opposite corner. Seven point three five one metres. I send a wave down the tape. It unhooks and whips back, scraping at the grouting between the bricks. That's two millimetres longer than the last time I measured it. I look up at the house. —This better be a mistake, I say.

Once inside I see my sister is extending her range. She is back in her corner but the top of her backpack is edging off the sheet. A piece of charcoal is beyond its borders entirely, lying three and a half centimetres away at an angle of fifty or so degrees to the sheet's hypotenuse. I decide not to measure it: she will see it, she will pick it up and put it back on the sheet. It's a temporary formation which will soon pass.

I pad through the rooms, flicking off the lights. I check the dimensions of the supporting walls from the inside, which I have not taken since my initial scoping. None match the original data. The difference is a few millimetres, sometimes more, sometimes less. This is disconcerting. After remeasuring four times with no variation I can only assume I was initially sloppy. The other, more likely, possibility is that the house has changed. Entertaining this theory I have the urge to blame my sister. Her displacement. There is something Archimedic about the space she needs.

I stand up and let the tape measure retract. Or it could just be the drought.

Later I heat up a microwave meal for one. My sister comes into the kitchen, brushing her teeth.

—How can you eat that stuff? she asks through the toothpaste, taking a glass from the cupboard and holding it under the tap.

I show her the box.

—It has all my daily requirements, I say.

She smiles, her toothbrush gripped between her teeth, and turns the tap off with a clunk.

—If only that were true, she says.

I accidentally laugh.

It's not that I dislike her company. It's just that it can't be contained: not in space and not in time either. She flashes me back. The quiet of my house is fissured with the noise, heat and light of the past. In the map room I stand in front of my draftboard but can only see the motel room where she left me. The first morning without her, the room stuffy and crammed with the sound of trucks braking at the intersection nearby. I had the bedspread twisted around my ears and eyes, but could not block it out. I remember getting up, going outside, and finding the day already hot, the brightness of the light and colour beyond anything I was used to. Like a painting, like something fake.

At the traffic lights I stood still with the trucks rolling in towers past me, their wheels level with my line of sight. I wondered which of these poisonous six-lane roads she had taken. They looked exactly the same in all four directions, something that would never happen in my country, where roads were trodden, not planned. Nothing about the place was familiar, not the names on the road signs, not the make of the cars, not the rules that governed their movements. I had no idea where the roads led, where they came from. If you had shown me a map at that point I would not have been able to say where the motel was, where I was. So how would I ever escape? How would I know which of these identical, fume-filled roads to take? How did she?

When she goes to bed it is easier. The air stills, clears, and I can breathe again. I turn off the kitchen light and relax in the brief period of utter blackness my contracted pupils allow. Our eyes don't get used to the dark, she was wrong about that. Our eyes widen to the light within the dark. You can't stop them. In this shutterless country the yellow blur from the street lamp seeps in through the blinds, bringing with it all the vagaries of vision. But even blindfolded I would know the number and angle of my steps to get me safely to the draftboard.

The map lies open. I stretch my arms wide and grasp the edges of the wood. The paper flutters as I breathe out. In the minimal light the meaning of the map is obscured, but it's like a foreign language—the subject and object of its lines can be sensed. Despite its omissions and inaccuracies there remains a harmony, a pace, a rhythm to its markings which rings through my arms. I slide my right hand under the draftboard, raise the headlamp to the surface and squeeze it on. The map lies open. And I am taken in.

Chapter 10

When I wake up the house settles into place. I tilt my head against the pillow and listen to the rasping of the wallpaper sliding into position, the snap of the beams adjusting their joints. My sinuses ache. I peer through the pain at the corner above my bed, watch it grind its three planes into a credible angle. I hear my sister breathe deep into her ribcage, sucking the air from the room. The blankets are pinning my feet in their hospital corners, I twist and kick at them, skid out of bed and pull open the bedroom door. Oxygen flows in from the corridor, cool and dark.

I went to get her, our mother, two days after the evacuation and bombing that had destroyed my workplace. The first reports were coming through on the radio that in the north they were killing anyone with names like ours, faces like ours. I called my sister first. Her phone was answered by a woman I didn't know, who didn't trust me and wouldn't say if my sister was there. Who would only take a message: that my sister should come to my apartment, that I would get our mother, that we would all leave together if we had to.

I chose the more expensive method of travel: flying. I wanted to avoid as many checkpoints as possible; I didn't think they'd arrest me at the airport, I expected the systems of law and order to be better respected there than at the roadblocks. I could pass as long as no one checked my papers and found my name alone unacceptable. My skin and bone structure are ambiguous, I have middle-class clothes and an educated accent. I could look as if I were someone else, came from somewhere else.

As the plane came in to land I put on lipstick, jewellery and a pleasant expression. I was detained for two hours, but not tortured. I sat neatly with my hands in my lap as they questioned me. I told the truth. I wanted to get my mother and get out of there. At that stage I thought they'd accept it, that they just wanted us gone.

When I told them where my mother lived they laughed and let me go.

At work here I follow the progress of the Global Map from my relatively lowly position. I have nothing to do with it of course, though my level of participation on the project in my own country and my ability to speak about it authoritatively are probably what got me this job. Today the project manager for the Map in this country manages to run into me as we leave a meeting. He sighs and recounts the difficulties of collating datasets made with different methodologies and at different times, or complains of the gaps in detailed maps for this vast country. I help where I can, veiling my advice in indirect terms, to protect his ego. I want a promotion.

These encounters always end the same way, like a ritual. He shakes his head and comments on how difficult it must be for me to have lost all that work. I don't say what I am thinking: that there are greater things to lose. It would only embarrass him, and he is making an effort. We talk about the holes in the Global Map which persist, despite the best efforts of the International Steering Committee to share resources and skills.

Holes representing war, or poverty, or both. But it always comes back to the map of my country, how this is the most frustrating, as it is widely known how close the project was to completion. I go through the whole conversation feeling the memory stick scratch at my skin under my clothes.

It's not that I have become scientifically ungenerous. I just have the feeling that this is not the right time. That if I let go of this data now it might be misused, it might be taken from me, I might lose it forever. But I don't know what I'm waiting for. I don't know what it is, exactly, I'm hanging on to.

Perhaps it gives me a sense of power.

Back home I work on scaling in the sub-map of the bowl, refiguring it in its appropriate place on the map of the mantelpiece. I work with a sense of failure, knowing I am not capturing everything, knowing that every measurement seems to be, since my sister's arrival, a matter of interpretation. But I need to find a way to continue with this process, despite its inconsistencies, because I need to create something meaningful, something which will enable me to understand this place. There is so much unaccounted for. I have not yet managed to map what my eyes can see, let alone the boundless intricacy of what they cannot. But I am getting somewhere surely. I must be, because I'm moving forward, because every day is an addition to the map.

Chapter 11

The town that we grew up in, the town where my mother still lived, was bombed, while I was in the air on my way to find her. That's why the airport soldiers were laughing. The fleeing refugees were fired upon by snipers who waited for them, knowing they would come and which roads they would have to take. The massacre was condemned internationally, though if you didn't see the morning news here that day you would have missed it. There were a lot other acts to condemn by the evening cycle.

It was being discussed by two men standing next to me outside the airport, after the soldiers had let me go, as I waited for the bus. A bus to a town that no longer existed: something that they knew and I didn't. I listened in to their conversation, receiving fragments of information like ice cubes to the spine. Until I had to interrupt. They seemed to take some pleasure in telling me about it, in making the link to the cancellation of the bus service, or perhaps it was just their own shocked disbelief coming out in nervous laughter. —It's hard to tell. In any case, they said, —it's not safe to travel. The taller of the two looked at me closely. —Not for someone like you, he said.

I didn't listen. I spent two days getting around whichever way I could, hitch-hiking, walking, relying on the sympathy of strangers or at least their apathy. I got as close as I could to the bombed town without having to confront soldiers. I was looking for information, trying to find out what had happened to anyone who might have survived. The general consensus was that not many could have, and those who did could be anywhere, trying to get to relatives or friends, or just hiding out in the surrounding area. You wouldn't find them, though, if they had any sense.

In the end I got a flight back south, thinking perhaps my mother had been trying to call, or come. I only realised later, in my apartment, watching the news, how lucky and how stupid I had been.

I was still safe, despite sharing ethnicity and origin with the people getting killed. It kept nagging at me, the fact that I was still safe, over those next few weeks before it all got too bad to stay, before my sister finally arrived and we left. I was still safe, here in my furnished flat, safe in my southern city with my middle-class job, safe watching the reports of what was happening to those who didn't share my security. I was still safe, for the moment at least, because I was not where I should have been, because I wasn't in the right place at the wrong time, because I had somehow escaped the stereotype and could no longer be seen for what I was. For weeks I couldn't get the image of the old people out of my head. I kept seeing pictures of them, flicking over and over like the end of a reel, the old people stumbling down the hill to get out of the town, their knees painful, their progress slow. Targeted as much for where they lived as who they were. Their guilt cartographic. I couldn't help but feel implicated.

And still I expected a call from my mother, with some extra-ordinary story of escape, or better still about how she had been visiting friends in another, safer, town, but couldn't get to a phone until now because of this reason or that reason. As time went on, the story had to be adjusted in my mind, the reasoning became less and less probable, until at last my reasonable self could no longer accept its plausibility.

The database of the relocated, set up by humanitarian agencies to allow survivors to find relatives and friends, has a certain hope to it, even amid the names of strange countries and towns, the vast distances implied. There are people on that database that I might one day see again, should I want to. As for the database of the dead, it has, at least, a finality. It allows for the possibility of mourning, the experience of loss which, despite its pain and magnitude, forms a sort of foundation upon which you can rebuild.

But the database of the missing has no such quality. It is defined by the absence of the people on it; it is not so much a storehouse of information, but of its lack. When we put my mother in such company, some months later, it felt like locking her away, committing her to an asylum where she would exist stateless, like Schrödinger's cat, neither alive nor dead. It requires of us, to this day, an exhausting sort of suspension, like having to hold a position, like having to balance all our thoughts about the situation, all our analyses, theories, emotions, in some complicated, precarious formation, constantly poised to tip into grief, or, less probably, joy. I now find myself not caring how things fall. Just so long as they do.

Chapter 12

The house is lit up from where I stand, six metres from the façade. The illusion is that if you take one more step you might arrive. The front window reflects the light of my headlamp, I have my retractable tape measure laid out in a perpendicular trail to the front wall, and I embody Zeno's dichotomy paradox. I will move forward three metres, which means three metres will remain. Then I will move forward half of that, one point five metres, leaving another one point five. Then half of that again, point seven five, and so on. I will keep moving forward but, asks Zeno, how will I ever reach my house when half of the previous distance always remains?

I end up with my nose and toes to the brick of course. I am of finite size, which eventually means immense. I rest my forehead on the wall and calculate the distances I cannot step because of my mountainous feet. When my sister puts her head out the window I try to explain. All she can ask is why I expect to be infinitely small. I turn my forehead against the bricks to look at her.

—Don't you think you've missed the point? I ask.

She grins.

—Maybe not, maybe the enormity of humanity is a hint.

I search her expression for any trace of irony. She's pleased with something, but I doubt it's humanity. I come inside anyway.

A more likely possibility, from my limited understanding of modern mathematics, is that the sum of an infinite number of consistently decreasing distances can be finite. If so, this suggests to me that I should be able to map my house, not only in infinite detail, but also within a finite period of time. My calculus skills aren't up to confirming this theory. I will need to talk to a mathematician.

On my way into work the next morning the shopfront television set is again showing its mislabelled map of my country. I cup my hands around my eyes and peer through the window. What upsets me is not, as would be expected, the fact that the news network has got a map of my country wrong. What upsets me is the niggling uncertainty that the error instils: the irrational fear that they might have got it right. I recognise that this is achieved through the sheer force of their graphics, the confidence of their presentation, and the ubiquity of their broadcasting. I understand that I should not allow myself to doubt everything I know on the basis of such superficial tricks. But it forces me to imagine that my home might not be where I thought it was. I push myself away from the window. Whether through negligence or design they have the power to do this: displace an existing understanding; make an exile of knowledge.

But I know the cartography of my country better than they do, better, no doubt, than anyone else still alive. I had a reputation at home. I was allowed into the national map depository even during the war, when all public buildings were closed. The political geography of the north was collapsing, people were fleeing south or directly to the coast. I remained in the city because I was waiting for my sister. The phones were no longer working in her region, but she must have got the message, and had sent a letter with her expected arrival date. She was bringing another woman, and a child. Though I didn't admit

50

it to myself, in the most practical part of my mind I had already stopped waiting for my mother.

In the depository the one remaining worker gave me everything I asked for. I had come to know him over the years and he laid out the relevant maps at my favourite table. The rarer items in the collection had already been shipped out of the city, he explained, and he was trying to secure the rest as best he could. I took up my dividers and pencil. The borders had been realigned, and as I could no longer access any of the official, electronic versions, I would have to make the alterations here. But the librarian stopped me. He was polite, almost deferential, but insistent. He understood, he said, but there really was no point.

And so I went back outside, out of the peace and order of the library and into the unbelievable streets. The bullet-pocked buildings, the smashed and looted shops. People sobbing at bus stops, still trying to live their lives within an infrastructure that had become a mockery of itself, with all structure gone. A man in uniform coming around the corner, the sight of him making me change direction, go down a side street, get out of his sightline as quickly and inconspicuously as possible. Everything was conditional on the politics of that particular day: on who you were, on who they were, on who you were to them. I don't know what scared me most: the international forces interested in our protection or the soldiers of our country interested in our defence.

The problem was finding the end point, knowing at exactly what stage the war had become a direct danger to you, knowing when you should stop trying to live your life and start running for it. I was looking, but I couldn't see it. I didn't notice when the line had been crossed and I still couldn't tell you exactly when it was. I just knew I wasn't leaving until my sister arrived.

But it had been crossed. And I was still there that same night, sitting up in bed in the dark, shocked out of sleep. Listening to the knock on my apartment door, breathing high in my throat.

Then I thought it might be her.

Part Two

FUGUE

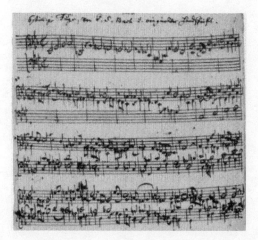

12.5

The sister. In the other country, the past, outside the house of rooms. She stands at the end of the vegetable patch, which is long and thin and stretches the entire length of the neighbouring field. It is bare under the late winter sky, ploughed and waiting for spring. The women don't know if they should plant it out or not, given the war. Maybe they'll have to leave.

She starts running. Through the clods which crumble under the slam of her sneakers. She starts running thinking only of the jump. The women watch, their pockets full of seeds. The end of the vegetable patch is crossed by a stream. The sister reaches it and takes flight. She is airborne for only a short time, far shorter than she expected. She comes down on her right foot with a splash at the stream's opposite side. The women clap and laugh.

The discussion as they go back to the house is about whether they should plant the seeds anyway in case the vegetables are needed in summer, by them or someone else. The woman who did the gardening gets to decide: she has already, over the years, planted the orchard, shade trees, a herb bed. Saying all the time this is not for us, this is for the future, which will be better than this because of what we've planted. She is calm now, philosophical, considering what's at risk. She says that whether you plant depends on your attitude to hope. —Is it hope that you will continue, or simply that something will?

—Something, answers the sister's lover. —But not just anything.

The sister's lover. Knows where everything is, what must be done next and what must be prepared in advance. Lives in several time zones, the present, the immediate future and tomorrow, because she has a child, a job and a cause. A not-yet-lost but currently losing cause. She is a member of a group that has come to be seen as a threat, not merely dissenting but seditious, treacherous, the irony being that they always were. She does the dishes with another woman, who—only now, only in this climate of suspicion and violence, only now that they are all scared—asks her how she could do this to her son. The sister's lover answers how can she not do this for him? And quotes the Count of Monte Cristo: Treason is a matter of dates.

Not just anything, thinks the sister, in the high room where she paints, her right foot wet and cold in her sneaker. She picks up a brush but has trouble visualising the arc, the form of what she wants to do. She fears she will fall short. She looks into her canvas like an oracle, doesn't see the brushstrokes or the stuck bristle or the white threads showing through the gaps. Sees instead only the potential of it, as if she might find something there, as if it might tell her something. Give something back for all this effort, according to the natural law of reciprocity, of which the canvas is unaware.

The woman who made the pots had warned her that you can't bring everything through. That you have to be satisfied with imperfection, incompleteness. She showed the sister how to cup the clay, how to shape it in her hands. Just see what you can bring through, she said. Bring through to form.

In the rooms around and below her some of the women have started packing.

Chapter 13

The house is lit up when I open my eyes, but the sunlight does nothing to warm the icy air. The house is badly insulated, all warmth seeps out through the walls and floor. I sit up and pull the quilt around my shoulders. In her sleep my sister's breath fogs. She is curled in a trilobite spiral at the foot of my bed, the sleeping bag's hood pulled tight over her head.

When I get to work I stop by the office of a mathematician colleague and ask her about Zeno's paradox. She's frowning at her computer screen and doesn't look up straight away.

—Hang on a sec, she says, clicking her tongue at what I suppose is an email. She shoots off a reply, hits 'send' then swings her chair to face me. She looks straight at me, holding eye contact a little too long, the way they do here.

I look away, around the room, taking in the papers and books on her desk, the calendar on the wall, the under-watered pot-plant in the corner.

—It's lovely really, she says. —Zeno, I mean. The so-called paradox.

She pauses until I look back at her.

—There's a formula, she continues. —Look.

She turns over an envelope on the desk and rummages in a drawer for a pen. I lean over her desk and turn my head to read what she's writing. She is left-handed, and hooks her wrist above the point where the pen touches the paper so as not to smudge the ink.

—Imagine that the first distance you cover is one metre, she says. —So the next distance is half a metre, the one after that a quarter of a metre and so on. She writes the figures $1 + \frac{1}{2} + \frac{1}{4}$, followed by three dots. She looks up at me to see if I'm following. I nod.

—All right, she says. —So you can actually make that into quite a simple algebraic formula—which someone eventually did—and it adds up to a finite number. I blink as she taps the pen against the paper to emphasise each point.

—Which number? I ask.

—Two.

—Two?

—In this case—which makes sense because we started with one and that was half way.

—So that means the distance can be covered in a finite time?

—Yes.

—Regardless of the infinity it contains?

—Good, isn't it? She smiles up at me. I push back from the desk to straighten up and increase the distance between us.

—But why is it possible? I ask. —Why does it work?

—Why? She laughs. —Because the maths shows us it does. And because we do it all the time—look.

She pushes her chair back from her desk so that it rolls to the wall behind her and slaps her hand against the plaster, grinning like she's won a race.

—So infinity is not an obstacle? I ask.

She raises her eyebrows and tilts her head. —Now there's a question. But not in this case. There's no real paradox with Zeno—at least not in the way it first seems.

I hold the edge of her desk between my finger and thumb, note the thickness of about one and three-quarter centimetres. She grabs its opposite side and pulls her chair back in.

—Why do you need to know about all this anyway? she asks.

They have no hesitation in posing direct and personal questions here—it's cultural. I let go of the desk and let my arms fall to my sides.

—No reason, I say.

She gives me a look of amused suspicion, reminding me of the women from home, at my sister's place.

Back in my office I look at the number series on the back of the envelope I have taken with me. Infinite intervals adding up to a finite distance. I could start with one straight line from the draftboard to an outer wall, then repeat the process through a series of radii, sweeping the house like the hand of a clock.

Chapter 14

When I arrive home the house looks ready for a fight. It crouches in waiting for me under the overcast sky. I walk straight up to it, slide the key into the lock, open it up. I have a methodology. It cannot get the better of me now.

I walk through the rooms, turning off the lights. My sister is out and the space is calm: a presence without a past. I drink my glass of water in the kitchen. Wash the glass, dry it, replace it. My heart beats the rhythm of each movement I make. From the drawer I take a hammer and a ball of string. In the map room I feel light-headed. I am dealing with infinity. I will conquer ambiguity. My map will be the first of its kind.

I drive a nail through the Point of Beginning, leaving the head to extend a centimetre above the slope of the draftboard. The hole in the heart of the blank rectangle widens; the copper wire is crushed through to the other side. I hear it tinkle onto the floor. The existing map winces inwards, buckling micro-scopically under this new attack. I brush my palms along its surface, from nail to corners, smoothing it back into place. It glows in the light from my headlamp.

The reasonable thing to do would be to pull it up, throw it out, lay down a new sheet and start again. It would give a clearer, more coherent result. But it disturbs me that such a result would be at the expense of a certain honesty: that such a result would require a disowning, a denial of past work, no matter how clumsy it may have been. Instead I will overlay the existing contours with the Zeno measurements. I will use a different pencil, a dark purple to contrast the deep grey of my previous efforts. I realise I am a perfectionist of process. I hope it won't slow me down.

I tie the string under the nail's flat head and push the knot down to the paper so that the string originates from the Point of Beginning at the centre of the map. With my compass in hand I roll the ball out to the window, find horizontal with a simple builder's level, then drive another nail into the window sill where it corresponds to the height of the Point of Beginning. I spike the ball of string onto it, twist until the string is pulled taut and fix it with a slip knot: due south and perfectly level. It traces a perpendicular to the draftboard's width, aligned east-west, and creates an angle to its downward slope.

The CD tray slides out at the press of my finger. I put on a medium-paced baroque canon and select 'repeat.' It will help me maintain rhythm and speed. Lights off, headlamp on, tape measure in pocket, tools strapped to wrists. Goggles ready on the draftboard for when I get into the small stuff.

I stand side-on to the Point of Beginning and count out the bars of the music, working out the steps for each measurement. The extension of the tape measure along the string is half a bar, finding the mid-point and marking the string another half. Half a bar to pull the levelling rod to the mark, another to drop the plumb line and check the vertical, another half to measure the depth. One whole bar for calculating elevation and marking it on the map, leaving the final half bar free. To enjoy the result. I wait for the start of a new phrase then start mapping. It's a formal dance of a methodology, as relaxed and inevitable as the swing of a metronome.

I do not lift my head from string, to ruler, to calculator, to map as my focus decreases. The house disappears and there is only the measuring of the house. The measuring and the music beating it out. I shuttle along the string and feel the air part for me, viscous as liquid. This is the way forward. It will take years, possibly decades. But what matters is that it is possible, which means there is an end point, which means I am getting somewhere, which means I can keep going. I feel exhilarated. There is the certainty of resolution; coming towards me as I move forward. It washes over me. This cartographic relief.

Chapter 15

The house is lit up when she arrives home. She bangs on the door shooting sparks through the floor, sending vibrations down the string which blurs and scatters the light from my headlamp. I am in the middle of a phrase and have to ignore her, continuing through the steps, in time with the music, until I have completed the measurement and marked it on the map. She knocks the whole time. I take off my goggles, pause the music and with it my whole methodology. —Let me in, she shouts.

Just when I felt I was getting somewhere.

At the front door she pushes past me, flicking on the lights, waving a newspaper, saying it's like home before the war how can they be so stupid. She has been to a protest, she has turned into a protest, she is all objection and dispute. As if I didn't have my own annoyances and frustrations, what with the mapping and her disruption of the mapping. But she has to bring more in. Politics, media, what some commentator said, what law was passed, she has to keep adding to the anger in the house until it glows, until the air twists inwards with it, until my skin dries in its pull.

I refuse to get sucked in. I flick off the lights behind her and go back to the point on the radius where I left off. There is no point trying to continue with this new methodology while she's here to upset its rhythm. I will work instead on correcting the inaccuracies I found earlier.

As she will not stop talking I put in earplugs. They are far from perfect, but I'm counting on their symbolic value—zero as it turns out because she's not looking. Her voice comes through muffled and disjointed, which simply augments the incoherence of her argument. She starts on about war and how it happens, which leads her to home, which leads her to family and friends dispersed, missing, dead. She won't let it go and can't seem to see how it irritates me, how I need it like a hole in the head. What can she possibly expect me to say?

—Anything, she shouts. —I just want to know I'm not talking to a wall.

I take the earplugs out and hold them an inch from my ears.

—If it doesn't matter what I say, then why don't you just talk to a wall?

She flings the newspaper into her corner and goes to the kitchen. I twist the earplugs back in. I know she's upset and doesn't mean to annoy me. But I am only just managing to stay afloat in this sea of my own problems. It would be too much for me, the whirlpool of her emotion and experience. I would get pulled under. I would get dumped.

I curl my palms around the string, so fine it is barely sensible. Only the slightest burning sensation between my fingers as I slide sideways back to the draftboard. I unhook its end from the Point of Beginning and temporarily loop it on the window sill behind me so that I can stand in front of the draftboard and check my progress so far. The new purple points of measurement extend in a single line down from the white rectangle representing the map, the first at some distance away, the remainder getting closer and closer together as they approach the parallel lines of the window.

I clip my goggles over my eyes, collapse my focus as small as the lenses will allow. I go into diminution I go in in in until my sister and her arguments are too far away to matter. I am in with my contours like tiny waves, they lap at the borders of things, they are the borders. They sweep up, they curve, they are exponential. There is so much of the map still curled up, waiting, coming. It is unfinished like a symphony in movement.

Then the overhead light comes crashing in, washing out my lines. I tilt my head up to see, through the blur of my goggles, the outline of my sister in the doorway, her hand to the switch which she then plunges back down into darkness. I return my eyes to the map and she flicks it back on. I pull off the head-lamp and goggles in one movement and glare at her.

—Is that annoying? she asks.

—Very.

—Good.

There's more than anger in her eyes. There's water. —Can't you talk to me for five minutes? she says, and I realise she's on the brink of some emotional tsunami. She's just waiting for a reason and my continued silence would be one.

—All right, I say. —What do you want to talk about?

—All this, she says, waving vaguely at the newspaper and then, as if another thought has hit her, at me. —Everything that's happening, she adds.

—But why? I ask. —Things happen, or not, regardless of whether we discuss them.

—That's not true, she says, rubbing her face. —There are always things that can be done.

I search my mind for a sentence, something to satisfy her, to pacify her, so that she'll leave me alone.

—So do them.

It's the best I can come up with. I know I should concentrate or there'll be tears, but the map is magnetic and draws the eye in. She says, —I do, in response to what I can't remember. I place my fingertips on the draftboard.

—Is five minutes up yet? I ask.

—No.

She starts pacing, she circles the room anticlockwise, pulling the air in her wake. I instinctively hold on to the corners of my map. She stretches out her right hand brushing the walls and the window as she passes, the shelves, my folders, my books. She says —Can't you see? Can't you see?

—Five minutes is up, I tell her.

She slows down, puts more weight on her right hand, leans into the walls and funnels into her corner. Standing on the sheet, her back to the junction of the two walls, she folds her arms and stares at me. The air slows like water. I put the goggles back on and go into the map. Into it like it is my house, a house where I am alone, where I can walk through the rooms without taking a step.

It is so like the physical house it is easy to forget where you are. But what distinguishes it is the absence of a map on the draftboard. Here there is just a blank rectangle. It's a blatant lie, of course, but reassuring in its own way. It means the inaccuracies of the map are not reproduced and, inevitably, multiplied on the map of the map. And because the map of the map would itself need to be mapped, and so forth ad infinitum, accuracy could only diminish until nothing meaningful was left. The telescoping potential of misrepresentation, or rather underrepresentation, is thus avoided by the methodological surrender of this tiny white rectangle. But it pains me nonetheless. Tonight I can't even look at it.

I shift my eyes sideways to the blanked-out corner, but through the earplugs the clearness of the space is punctured by sounds: zips being undone, rummaging, a sigh. She makes her presence felt even here, in the map house, like a haunting. I hear her footsteps across the empty room, the tap running in the empty kitchen, her footsteps back.

This is not as disconcerting as it seems. The gap between representation and reality is comprehensible, unavoidable, and therefore, surely, forgivable. A mere side-effect of the process, which could be seen as the process of closing the gap. I need simply to maintain pace, adopt a methodology of sheer stubbornness, refuse to lose direction or have it lose me. —You haven't led me this far just to abandon me? I ask the map. My sister says, —What? Her voice comes out of nowhere but I don't look up, I stay in the map house. I say —I wasn't talking to you.

I move my eyes from my sister's paper corner, pass through the wall and am in the corridor. In cartographic projection the corridor is undoubtedly the most stunning landscape of the house. There is a sort of formal deformation to the floorboards as they stretch away from the front door, rolling like dunes, swirling occasionally in finger-print spirals, rising in tiny peaks. The contours here invoke a sense of peace unmatched by the rest of the structure, invisible to the naked eye. What's strange is that, in the physical house, the corridor is ugly and oppressive. It feels unresolved, as if it were still trying to achieve something with its architecture. The irregularity of its planes hard on the eye: six rough parallelograms which completely fail to mirror each other.

I have always felt there is something unusual about this cartographic contradiction. Not necessarily wrong. More that the corridor has resisted the mapping process in some way, that something has been missed, misinterpreted, or is perhaps not even scalable. I have never been able to put my finger on it.

When my eyes return to the map room of the map house, I notice something has changed. A note has been skewered to the nail at the Point of Beginning, as big as the borders of the rectangle representing the map. I adjust the focus of my goggles. It says: Can I have another five minutes? I unclip the goggles and lift my head. She is there.

She reaches forward and pulls out my earplugs.

—Is that what this is all about? she says.

—What?

—Abandonment? You think I abandoned you?

—What? Come on. I said I wasn't talking to you.

—I don't need to justify myself to you.

—No, I say.

—And you have no right to hold it against me.

—No.

—Then why do you?

—As I said, I wasn't talking to you.

—You hardly ever are, that's the problem.

I shrug. Whose problem? I think.

—I mean I'm here now aren't I? she says.

—Yes you are.

She rolls the earplugs between her palms.

—Well, she says. —Can't you just be my sister?

—Done.

—You know what I mean.

—I have no idea what you mean.

She stares at me.

—Forget it then, she says.

—Can I have my earplugs back?

She hesitates then holds out her two closed fists.

—Guess, she says.

I focus the headlamp on her right hand, she opens her palm. Empty. —Left then. She smiles, opens one finger after the other. Also empty. I grip her wrist and slide my fingers under the cuff of her shirt, hook out the earplugs.

—I taught you that, I remind her.

—I know, she says. —That's what I mean.

She picks up the remote control for the music system which is still lying on the draftboard and flips it in her palm. Half a turn, a full turn, two full turns. I watch her, trying to read her intentions, her mood, to imagine what she might do next. When she goes for three turns she misses the catch. The remote bangs against the edge of the draftboard and the music starts up again, from the middle of my interrupted canon. I pick it up, stop the music and put the remote back in its place on a shelf.

She had done that in the motel room before she left— tossed things up and down in her hands, before thrusting them into her backpack. Pots of hand cream, shoes, a portable alarm clock. Like she was assessing their shape, volume, the limits of what she had, the vague idea of what she wanted.

I put my earplugs back in and go back to the map. That's when I should have said it—before she zipped up her backpack and turned to go. I should have said I waited for you for three days. I waited with people shouting in the corridor, with bombs blasting the surrounding buildings to rubble. As if my waiting had a weight that could be held in one hand, and her need to leave in the other. As if that counted. As if there were a scale upon which such things could be counted.

15.5

Most of the women have left now. When the roads were still safe, or at least safer than they would later become. The woman who got things done had worked out what they should take, what they should abandon and what they should hide in case they could come back later. She shut down the communications, would let no one use the phone to call out, and gave no names, no clues, no indications to anyone who called in. Just took a message for the sister, from her twin.

The woman who made the pots buried her favourites deep in the vegetable patch. The woman who did the gardening followed behind her, planting out the seeds.

When the first group of women went to leave someone said that what they were missing was a woman who knew where to go. A woman who made maps. The sister realised then that she needed her twin, if either of them were to survive. She wrote four identical letters, asking the women to post them from different places, hoping that one of them would get through. Telling her twin she was coming.

The news reports have been getting worse and worse. The women who are still in the house are determined to stay, or resigned to it. The lover had wanted to wait in order to get information about certain members of her group, but two days have passed and she can find no way to communicate with any of them. —Did we ever exist? she asks the sister on the last night. —Or did I just dream it?

The sister is woken by the sound of her lover's son throwing a tennis ball against a wall somewhere below their bedroom. She opens her eyes, her eyelashes brushing the neck of her lover, who, feeling the eyelashes, turns towards her, like an exhalation, with ease and grace. She pulls the sister in close and the sister breathes the smell of her lover's hair and face and skin soft as the sheets.

The sister knows that now is not a good time to leave, but that all the better times have passed. That leaving is probably the worst thing to do, but that all other options have been exhausted. She makes breakfast in the kitchen, pours the remainder of the oats into a plastic bag, knots the end. The lover takes it, her son watching them both, worried that they are worried. They pack their backpacks with food, passports, a few clothes and all their money. The sister leaves her paintings behind.

Their progress is slow, weighed down as they are, and because of the need to go unnoticed. They try to stay among trees where they can, because even though there are no leaves, the trunks and branches are a sort of shield. Sometimes they have to bolt across a bare field. They sleep hidden in a wooded area between two familiar towns, with the sleeping bags wrapped around each other, for warmth. The next morning, cold and blue, they eat red kidney beans from a tin and pack up, brush the dirt off the sleeping bags, trying to keep the leaves and sticks from getting rolled up inside.

The boy is tired and wants to complain but can see the atmosphere is wrong. When the child came with the lover, the sister made all the mental and emotional efforts required. She had never wanted children, but found something charming in

72

his fascination with small things: insects, mashed potatoes, a bike helmet. His harmlessness, perhaps because harmlessness is so rare. She didn't believe it could last, at least not in these circumstances.

She helps him put his backpack on, adjusts the straps so it doesn't pull so much on his shoulders. She feels a blister on her left foot, which rubs against the top of her sneaker as she buries the tin under a clump of long grass. The lover has a pain in her ankle which she broke as a child. She looks at it before putting her socks on. It's swollen and red. They check they haven't left anything behind and start walking.

They have to avoid the towns and the roads into towns until they get to the south. There are soldiers or pseudo-soldiers at the road blocks and they want to see identification before deciding how to treat you. The ethnicity of the sister's and lover's names will be acceptable for the pseudo-soldiers, who will assume solidarity because they have similar names, but not the official ones, who will assume enmity because they don't. And the lover's name is not only unacceptable but actually on a list for the official soldiers, she has been told, and possibly also for the pseudo-soldiers because the group the lover was associated with disagreed greatly on important points with the groups who have funded the pseudo-soldiers.

They have a map but it's of roads not the landscape itself, and when they do cross roads they can't find signs to identify them. They get lost. They find a wooded area that a farmer has left as a windbreak and sit hidden by fallen branches. They decide the sister will walk along the service roads until she can find a village and work out where they are. If it looks safe and if there is a shop open she will buy food, water, Band-Aids and paracetemol. She does all this, without getting caught.

When she comes back the lover and her child are gone. Just gone.

Chapter 16

When I wake up the house is dark. The silence outside tells me it's long before dawn. I have a sense of unease. The music I was mapping to earlier is playing in my head, but all sense of progression is gone. It loops over and over with a chilling familiarity, like it will never end. On the shadows of the bedroom ceiling I see the north line of the map, marked with the purple dots of the new measurements. There are none between the Point of Beginning and the first elevation, at the half-way point to the window. The density of dots increases closer to the window. But they never arrive. How can they arrive?

I go in to work early and wait at the café on the corner where the mathematician picks up her morning coffee. I buy it for her in exchange for five minutes. We sit at the counter near the steam from the machine, nodding at other colleagues as they file through. She looks at me with expectation and I realise I will have to tell her everything about the process if I am going to get any useful answers.

She doesn't take her eyes off me as I speak, spooning sugar into her latte by touch and stirring it for longer than is necessary. I tell her about using the string for the first radius and how the music ensures consistency of time for each measurement. I tell her that it started well but now I feel there's a lag to the process, that the points of measurement are getting closer to the end of the string but never arriving, that I don't think they can arrive, and that I think there is something wrong. When I stop she glances around the café, then looks back at me, frowning.

—Do you understand? I ask.

She raises her eyebrows. —Yes, she says, emphatically, with the upward intonation they use here that makes you doubt every single word. She takes a sip of her coffee, breaking her gaze and tapping her fingers against the counter. After a minute she looks back up. —Okay, she says, —there is a problem with what you're trying to do.

—Where? I ask.

—Pretty much everywhere, she says. Upward intonation again. —There's a big difference between mathematics and mapping.

—Look, I tell her. —Don't worry about the mapping. The problem is with the maths.

—No, the problem is with the mapping.

I breathe out. —Well I'm asking about the maths, I say.

—Then what's your question exactly?

—Why isn't it working? According to what you said yesterday, all the infinite points contained in the string add up to a finite distance, yes?

—Yes.

—And so I can move along the string, across all those points, in a finite period of time?

—Easily.

—So why wouldn't I be able to measure the elevation at each of those points and map them?

—Because passing through an infinite number of points is one thing, actively engaging with them is another.

—What do you mean?

—It's like counting them one by one.

I pause. I don't see the problem. —Why can't I count them one by one? I ask.

—Because there's an infinite number of them. The act of naming them means it would take, well—she waves her hand —an infinity.

She takes another sip of her coffee and looks at me as if waiting. I pick up my cup and put it down again. —But the formula counts them, I say.

—Yes, but the formula allows you to leap to the end so you don't get sucked in to dealing with each infinitesimal point. That's the beauty of it. That's why, as I said, the maths is not the problem.

She grins. I stare at her. I can see what she means.

One of her colleagues calls out to her from the doorway, pointing at his watch.

She drains her coffee and stands up. —I've got a meeting, she says.

—But then how can we move through them? I ask. Too loudly, I realise, as her colleagues pause in their conversation and look over. She ignores them and places her hand on the counter in front of me, deliberately, like a point of focus.

—It's not the same thing, she says. I look from her fingers to her face. Her smile is utterly genuine. She is actually enjoying this tragedy, or doesn't even recognise it as such.

—When we move, she continues, —we are, in a sense, more linked to concept than to counting. The formula leaps space and so do we. We don't have to go step by infinitesimal step.

77

She speaks like she's giving a lecture, with all the surety of someone who has nothing more to worry about than metaphysics.

—So it can't work, I say to her, more as a statement than a question. She tilts her head at me

—Look, the real problem with Zeno, she says —has nothing to do with moving through infinite points in space—that's a given, we do it all the time. The real paradox lies in the gap between what we can conceptualise in the abstract and what we can count and measure in concrete terms.

I look at her. She wraps her scarf around her neck and looks back at me.

—That in itself is pretty amazing, don't you think? she asks.

As if it were no great problem that I cannot find a methodology to properly chart the space I inhabit, as if that were of no significance at all. How am I going to get this done now?

She is still looking at me.

—Yes, I say. —Amazing.

Chapter 17

When I arrive home the house is lit up, the afternoon sun striking the front window so that it glares. My sister is out. In her corner the sun hits a still-life of potential movement—the plastic cup on the brink of tipping, the backpack crammed to ripping point, scrolls of canvas spilling from its openings in a frozen tumble. Like the rest of the universe, she cannot maintain order for long.

I stand with my toes to the fold of the sheet. I have an urge to kick, but why add to the disarray? Instead I kneel and pluck a canvas roll from the pile, taking care not to displace the others. A woman I don't know, leaning against a bench in some industrial-looking kitchen. A colleague from one of her jobs perhaps. I roll it up and replace it, taking another. A woman I remember from my sister's place at home, lying in the grass, reading, a boy crouched next to her with a caterpillar on his finger. I unscroll canvas after canvas on my lap. Women, and sometimes children, occasionally men. Now at a table, or in the garden at her place before the war, or on the streets of a city, which is perhaps my home, by the architecture, the style of the signage. Exaggerated, vague, all energy and no detail. Impressive, but ultimately unnavigable.

I take care to replace them in their original formation and push myself onto my feet. I can't get sucked into this ambiguity, it's like losing blood. I need precision, and momentum. I need to work. But how?

I take the end of the string from where it's looped on the window sill and fasten it back under the nail head of the Point of Beginning. Then I unhook the ball of string itself from where it is spiked onto the sill and wind it up, reeling myself in towards the map. I stop at a distance of a metre or so and swing the string in a slow 90-degree arc sideways, walking with it, maintaining the horizontal, until it is stopped by the slope of the draftboard. Then I go back the other way, 180 degrees, until I am stopped on the opposite side, near the kitchen door. I could adjust the draftboard so that it lies flat and continue in a full circle. Nothing stops me. I can move through it all, this infinity of space. But I can't get any traction on representation.

The knot grinds against the Point of Beginning as I swing the string one way then the other, as I swing with it. The problem is not so much methodological as instrumental, and my bluntest instrument is myself.

I stop near the window and look down at the ball of string in my hands. It isn't leading me anywhere. I finish winding it up, unknot it and remove it from the nail at the Point of Beginning. The last of the sunlight glances off the nail head. I tuck the string into my pocket and watch the nail's shadow lengthen along the map and start to fade. This is where it all starts, I remind myself. Think about it. This will determine how it ends.

I think about it, and it goes like this. Imagine that I were a perfect cartographer. Imagine that I could defy the mathematics and actually take an infinite number of infinitesimally small measurements in a finite period of time. Imagine that I could achieve an absolute delineation of this place in its every detail, that I could grasp it, capture it, disambiguate it in its totality. What then? What would my map look like, in the end?

The map goes dark as the last of the sun disappears below the horizon. It's simple. There will come a point where the drafting paper is saturated. Where the page will be so black with lead that no pattern can be perceived. Except this, I think, putting my finger to the gleam of the Point of Beginning. It will be a pinprick of light among the seep and entanglement of my lines.

I turn away and go into the kitchen, stand with my back to the inner wall. Have I always known this? That rigour of process would destroy it all? I put the string back in the drawer. Drink a glass of water. Wash the glass, dry it, replace it. Fold the tea towel over the oven door. I look for something else to put in order, but everything is in its place. I lean against the sink as the darkness crawls up my legs, the cupboards, the kitchen surfaces. The fridge shudders into silence.

17.5

The sister looks around under the branches, in the trench by the side of the road, pulls at the grass and the bark on the trees. Even words have gone missing. In any case there's no one to tell. She has no solidity, no liquidity, no property at all. She is stateless.

What she wants to do is scream, if it were explicable and acceptable and safe. What she wants to do is wail like the women who have lost children, husbands, to go back to the bombed out buildings they passed yesterday and search the rubble, uselessly, fruitlessly, throw bricks, slam her head against the chimneys which are always the last to fall.

Instead she considers the possibilities. One: she is in the wrong place. She retraces her steps back to the village, but the path is three-times familiar, she can feel it.

In the centre of the village she turns around. She feels as if she is being watched. The houses lining the square have no front gardens; their curtained windows twitch and are closed upon her. She shares ethnicity with the people here but she feels vulnerable nonetheless, as if the disappearance of her lover will expose her, expose the fact that she is not like them. And in that case, though they may not wish her harm, she would be last on the list of those they would help.

She goes back into the one shop which is still open, a bakery where she had bought bread two hours before. Had they seen a young woman and a boy, carrying backpacks? No. The sister has a sense of betrayal but she doesn't know whose. The warm smell of yeast makes her feel sick on each intake of breath. There seem to be no further questions she can ask.

Two: they left freely. To look for a stream to wash in, to drink from. But they wouldn't have taken their backpacks. To move to somewhere safer then; perhaps they saw someone and felt threatened. In which case they would come back to get her. So she should go back to the place where they are gone, and wait.

She does, and spends the night sitting on her backpack, hidden from the road, leaning into a tree. As the hours pass the wind rises into a gale. She looks up at the dancing branches. They bend their limbs randomly, as if the wind had no direction, only force, violence, the wood cracks, the branches break themselves against each other, fall around her. One bangs down on her knees. After a second she screams.

She doesn't think she sleeps but the night passes more quickly than is reasonable so perhaps she did. When she stands up she can't straighten her right knee, and sees her jeans are stuck to the skin with dried blood. She washes the gash with as much bottled water as she dares and binds it up with a T-shirt, then eats the bread she bought the day before. She limps forward and looks around. Up and down the road. They are still gone.

Three then. Soldiers took them.

Chapter 18

The house is dark from where I stand, my lower back cold against the kitchen sink. The gloom in the map room is more sombre than night, the heavy cloud outside blanketing the moon and muffling sound. The weather is turning; we are in a trough. There is a pressure in my head which, I hope, might precede revelation. I listen to my lungs, my arteries, the deep beat of my heart.

My legs have gone numb. I force myself to move, limping into the map room, trying to walk it out, bring sensation back. I just need to find where to pitch my imagination, where to aim in order to at least approach the perfect result I am hoping to achieve. I put on my headlamp and go through the house, looking for the theoretical ideal.

In the bathroom the porcelain is chilling. I line up the bottles of shampoo, soap, conditioner along the edge of the bath, labels facing out. At the extremes of infinite detail and infinite scope there is no meaning, or, at least, no representation of meaning. Reductio ad absurdum. I've been treating scale as if it were something that could not be compromised, a conceptual puzzle which, once resolved, would enable me to move forward. But perhaps scale is by nature compromise, perhaps compromise is, in cartographic terms, all there is.

Under the light of my headlamp I notice there are blooms of mould growing between the tiles. They spoke outwards and repeat themselves, trailing kaleidoscopically above the bath. I pull the shower curtain across to cover them. This doesn't matter, I tell myself. My concern is not the house, but the capturing of it.

I just need to focus. I just need to work with what I've got, start with what I already have and make decisions. I go back to the map room and stand in front of the draftboard. The map draws down my focus, pulls the light of my headlamp to it like gravity. I recognise that it is, for the moment, approximate. Inaccurate even. But look at it. It is passing through the most exquisite of forms. It is, in these early drafts, unique.

I tighten my dividers and ruler into the wristband, sharpen my pencil and check the regularity of its tip through my goggles. I examine at low magnification the purple droplets of my Zeno measurements as they drip south, collecting at the bottom of the page. The pearls of my failure. There is a beauty to this unfinished, imperfect effort. Perhaps compromise is not a defeat, but a consolation.

I just need to be able to recognise the point at which the pattern is maximised; the point just before form folds into nothingness or everythingness, before it is extended, or reduced, to banality. A form that will reference the paradox and contradiction of the process without being subsumed by it. What matters, in the end, is not how much it takes in, but how much it gives back.

Chapter 19

The house is lit up at my touch as I walk through the rooms in the deep of the night. I have been working for hours to the rhythm of my own breathing and that of my sister as she sleeps in the bedroom nearby. I am surrounded, I now realise, by a structure that exists at a level of complexity I have not even begun to grasp. Look at the way it resists the linearity of my processes, the way it shifts and changes with the weather, the light and its own inhabitants. Its dimensions are not only infinitely divisible, but barely determinable. They cannot be taken at face value. It's a miracle they ever add up at all.

I have left my instruments behind and am astounded by the senseless way in which I can measure without them. I meet fingertip to light switch without even thinking. How am I capable of such accuracy in such a short time: the curves, the vectors, the precision, the numberless miniature calculations, the adaptability of it? I turn the lights on and off. Am I that powerful?

I am stunned by the texture revealed. Plaster, wood grain, cloth, paper humming a bass line from which the architecture flies off. The falling chords of the bookshelves, the tempo to the walls. The pause of doorways. The sostenuto of skirting boards, the woodwind of the floorboards, air pushing through. The bathroom tiles climb in thirds.

The house is layered with detail, it is in augmentation,

there is a sort of momentum to the structure that takes off in unpredictable directions, like an escape, like flight.

The house is a fugue.

I crouch at the end of the corridor backed by its four corners behind my heels and overhead. At the other end I see the front door similarly framed in all these angles which are intimate to me. I realise I am no longer making sense. This is natural, considering where I live. What matters is not to make sense of it, but to chart it. To formalise, not analyse. What is analysis, after all, but a structured speculation, an attempt at approximation, a random simplification, a guess?

I follow the thought back to my map, itself a sea of woven strings. The straight, improbable lines of the scoped walls, the curled contours of floorboards and everything that stands upon them. I must continue adding detail, in smaller and smaller measures. I bring my ear to its surface. It should vibrate along its harmonics when touched with a fingertip or the point of my dividers. There is just one more line missing, one more layer I need to add, one more measure, one more decimal point. I am waiting for it to ring.

I arc my dividers along the shelves in swinging, measured steps. I have the sense of coming upon something, of forms in the distance coming into view. I have the impression of pattern, I have the feeling that pattern and progression are inextricable, that something must be revealed. The new starts to seem familiar. Look at the wood grain, how its knots repeat, look at the texture of the plasterboard, the ridges and ripples, look at the curves in the spines of my books. I rap my knuckles and hear a repetition of beams, invisible in the walls. I will capture this

87

pattern, I will crystallise form out of the ceaseless accumulation of complexity. I will make of my map a symbol which will allow me to see.

Chapter 20

The house is lit up from inside and out. The morning sun hits the windows and stripes through the closed blinds. I am lying on the map room floor, my headlamp aimed at the lit bulb in the centre of the ceiling. Wondering if I should be in the map. I know I'm a temporary formation, but I'm here now. The map is of what's here now. In the haze of my sleepiness it seems doable.

I shift sideways into an uninteresting space between the draftboard and the kitchen. I want a challenging formation, so I bend both knees and fold one over the other to create an overhang—always difficult for topographical representation. A viewer will take some time to work out what the resulting contour lines are saying. I'll have to do my arms last, because I need them. The map will be called Death of a Cartographer.

I take my callipers and stretch them wide to span the length of my head from chin to crown. I hear my sister open the bedroom door. From the corner of my eye I see her slippers shuffle by towards the kitchen. She puts the kettle on and comes back to the doorway, stretching up to grip the top of the frame. I do cheekbone to cheekbone and temple to temple, take the pencil from behind my ear and note the results on the Post-it slips stuck to my left hand.

—Do you want a coffee? she asks.

—I can't move right now.

—I'll make it.

—But I won't be able to drink it.

I shift my eyes to her and smile.

—You're in a good mood, she says.

—It's all coming together.

She's still in the long T-shirt she wears to bed, legs bare. I realise I haven't seen her knees in over twenty years. The strange thing is they haven't changed, except for a jagged scar on the right one. I look up at her face. It's always so much older than I expect it to be.

My arms feel heavy as I move through my measurements. When I close my eyes I feel myself slipping, frictionless, into sleep. My mind is still searching for my sister's younger face, her child's face, but can't find the memory. There are a series of doors, with rooms I can't get to because the doors in between are locked. I can hear the kettle whistling and my sister moving crockery but I am surrounded by doors which in the whistling fly open. I spin around and my sister is there; she grabs my wrist and pulls me through room after room, we end up running, from someone or to something; all I can catch are glimpses of people and rooms, I note the exits, how far away the doors and walls.

—So what's this? she says to me, loud and close, shooting adrenalin through my muscles. I force my eyelids open. She's standing at the window, waving her coffee cup in my direction. The callipers have fallen on to my face. I try to brush them off and search for the breath to form words. —Mapping myself, I say.

My sister sucks air in between her teeth. She steps over me and stands at the draftboard, her coffee cup hovering over the pencil trench at a perilous angle. I want to close my eyes to avoid looking at it, but sleep is waiting to ambush me.

—I thought you were mapping the house, she says. —You're not part of the house.

I force myself to sit up.

—I'm mapping everything starting with my draftboard and moving outwards, which encompasses me.

—But you won't always be here.

—I already explained this to you.

—I know, it's what's there when you take the measurements. But the thing is, taking the measurements takes a long time, doesn't it? And things change in the time it takes you to take the measurements.

—Which means the map is immediately out of date, I know.

—No, it's not just that. I mean, you're going to change position before you even finish the map, aren't you? You have to, in order to come over here and put yourself in the picture?

—I know.

—So that means your map's not only out of date, but that it's out of date in different ways in different places—you've got the blank rectangle for the map, for example, and then on the same map you're going to have you lying there on the floor, implying that you were there at the same time as the blank map, which is not the case, obviously, because the paper I'm looking at here isn't blank. You've never lain there while the map was blank, I'm supposing—do you see what I mean?

—It's blindingly obvious what you mean.

—What are you getting upset for?

This is useless. I put my pencil back behind my ear, pick up the callipers and get to my feet.

—If all you can do is point out methodological difficulties, I begin.

—Difficulties? More like a fundamental flaw in the process.

She's squinting at me and I realise my headlamp's still on. I switch it off and pull it from my head. She looks alert, cheerful. I don't think she means to irritate me. She has always been like this in the mornings.

—Could I have some coffee after all? I ask her, holding out my hand for her cup.

She purses her lips but gives it to me, and I immediately feel safer now that it's in my hands. I drink it in one go, feel the heat and the caffeine jolt through me. I prise myself between her and the map so that she steps backwards and hold out the empty cup. She tugs it from my hands and goes back into the kitchen.

Leaning into the lower edge of the draftboard I examine the map. She's right of course, but maybe I can add myself as an appendix. Or a pop-up? I should think about it when I'm less tired. And I can't concentrate with her constant interruptions.

She has spilt water from the kettle onto the hotplate; it hisses like a slow fuse.

—How long did you say you were staying? I call out.

I watch her over my shoulder as she comes back into the room with a refilled cup. She walks over to the mantelpiece. It suits her height; she rests her elbow on it, bends her arm up and leans her head into her hand.

—I wanted to talk to you about that, she says.

I just look at her. My instinct is not to move at all.

—I was thinking of getting a job, she continues. —Here, I mean. In this city.

I don't even breathe.

—But I need an address, you know, for correspondence. To show I'm stable.

—You can't stay here, I say.

I'm as surprised as she is at the way this comes out. I had intended to be more diplomatic. She frowns at me and wrinkles her nose.

—Have you slept? she asks.

Anger rises through me. I've lost so much time because of her.

—Look, you can't stay for the reason I gave you when you arrived. You're disrupting my work.

She opens her mouth. I think she's genuinely surprised.

—How?

—You're always making noise, I say. —It's distracting.

—I hardly ever make noise.

—You disarrange things.

—Everything I have is on that sheet. You're talking nonsense. If you have anything specific to ask of me, anything I can actually do something about, then tell me.

—Specific? Okay. These are the things you have done to block, hinder or disrupt my project since you arrived, I say. —Number one: being here, that is being, you know, yet another object in the environment. Two: bringing more objects into the environment, such as newspapers, food and the bowl. Three.

I have to look around and then I see it.

—Three: spilling that five-millimetre circle of green paint on the floor next to your triangle.

She drops her arms in frustration, the remainder of her coffee splattering onto the floor. I raise my eyebrows at her, but she turns away and goes into the kitchen. I follow her and open the cupboards and a drawer to make my next point.

—Four: moving a saucepan, a knife, a wooden spoon, two

93

plates and a glass and not putting them back in the right places.

She bangs her cup on the sink and goes back into the map room. I stay with her, pointing towards the bedroom.

—Five: leaving your clothes and sleeping bag in different formations every day.

—Look, just forget it, she says.

—Six: increasing the temperature and humidity of the house and therefore possibly changing its dimensions.

—I said forget it. You're being ridiculous.

—Seven: constantly interrupting me with banalities and preventing me from concentrating. Eight: suggesting facile solutions to complex problems, thereby distracting me and making me lose time. Nine: criticising various aspects of my methodology such as the validity of representing the map of the map as blank, or including myself in the terrain, yet offering no viable alternative. And ten: questioning the very value of the project itself.

She leans against the mantelpiece and rubs her face with her hand. —Okay, she begins and breathes in.

The coffee has done me a world of good. Things seem explicable.

—I think I have been extremely patient, I continue. —I have done everything I can to minimise your influence and make adjustments for it when I must. But it can't go on. There has to be an end point so that I can evaluate and repair the damage; get everything back to normal.

She has breathed in so far that her shoulders are near her ears. I remember a conflict resolution seminar from work and add, —This is important to me. I need you to respect that.

There is a silence while she breathes out. It takes several seconds. Then she drops her forearm along the length of the mantelpiece and curls her fingers around the bowl. She takes its weight, tilting and twisting her wrist so that the bowl pivots in the morning light. —You are blaming me for all your problems, she says.

She has missed the point again, as she always does, by thinking on the wrong axis.

—You are all my problems, I correct her.

There is a small disturbance between us, me expecting her to react and her suppressing a reaction. Then she lowers the bowl back onto the mantelpiece in a soundless, circular movement. The vibrations from her steps tap up my spine as she passes. She goes into the bedroom. To pack, I assume.

It's not like I wanted to do this. I'm not enjoying it, though she probably thinks it's revenge. She just has to go. She pulls me down from my legitimate processes, my bird's-eye perspectives. I land with a thump in the middle of her stupid landscapes.

I have to go to work. The caffeine has cleared my mind, but my limbs feel vague and dense. I think I'm at the draftboard; apparently my eyes have closed. I can't remember in what position I've left my body. I let my head fall back so that gravity opens my eyelids and try stretching my arms overhead. My right arm makes it up but not the left. I flop my head forward and see my left forearm lying along the pencil trench.

I have to go to work. There is a buzzing in the air, it circles me and eddies downwards through the floorboards. If I just lie down for five minutes I will be able to sort this out. Re-member myself. I kneel and curl myself under the draftboard. My eyes have closed again, but I'll keep my ears open. To the house.

I see her child's face on my closed eyelids, the hair pushed off it by a headband, her uncreased forehead exposed. The face that I had been unable to find, that I had lost, that was missing, that I have missed. We were so sure of each other then.

I know she's got nowhere else to go, but do I? This is my only place and I am only just coming to know it. And then she comes and pushes me, ceaselessly, without giving, without bending. She is unmalleable. She is so hard on me. My reaction is simply equal and opposite.

The house hums it rings it sings all its strings vibrating as I slip, this drop in the stomach like desire, like sleep. The beat of the floor suspends me, the melody of the ceiling overarches it. The north side of the house is muted by my sister, silent in the bedroom. I know she is keeping things from me. Secrets are always obvious.

20.5

When the woman in the bakery sees the sister again she closes the till and folds her hands in front of her abdomen. No, she still hasn't seen them. No, she hasn't seen any soldiers. A man comes in from the next room, brushing his floured hands on his apron. He looks the sister up and down. He heard there were soldiers going round the farms yesterday. Official soldiers. Looking for pseudo-soldiers and anyone who might have given them food.

Outside the sister feels watched. She walks past the church, the bar, her muscles tense in her neck and shoulders. The footpaths are narrow. She has to step into the gutter to pass the legitimate inhabitants. They will think there is something about her which is not right. There is nowhere to stop and nowhere to go.

Her problem is justified fear. If she goes to the official soldiers to report her lover and her lover's son missing and enquire whether they have been arrested, she knows that her name will make her guilty, worthless, someone to be punished. Then there is association, with the lover. The fact that she knows the lover's name and is looking for her. Another layer of suspicion. The best scenario, if she gets a certain soldier, or certain mood, or something's about to happen and they don't have time for her, the best scenario is that they just let her go. More likely is that they take her out the back and shoot her. Or rape and torture her and then shoot her. Or send her to one of the rape houses for the soldiers that are now rumoured to exist.

She tries, but she can't imagine a scenario in which they would give her information about the lover and child.

It's the apparent arbitrariness of their possible reactions which inspires something deeper than fear, which inspires a sort of giving up, a lack of expectation or even hope. Because how, after all, can she not go? How can she not take this risk even though she knows it cannot possibly achieve anything, how can she not do something, how can she not, just to be able to say she did everything she could? Does she want to be right, to act according to her principles, or is it just love and fear and panic? Upon what basis is she making her decisions now? This absurd feeling that if they could just be near each other things would be better.

The soldier is trying to sharpen a pencil over an ashtray but the sharpener is too big for the pencil tip. He pushes the pencil harder which breaks the lead and mangles the tip. The sister looks at him fascinated by his incompetence, the fact that this simple task is beyond him. She thinks maybe she will get out of here alive and unharmed after all; it gives her a deathly hope. He doesn't look up at the sister. When she gives her lover's name he drops the pencil and sharpener with exasperation and pulls a register from under the desk. —Date? he asks. —Yesterday, she says. He finds the name. The sister notices there is a circle next to it. Below is the boy's name. With a circle crossed diagonally by a line. The soldier looks up at the sister. —Relationship? he asks. —Cousin, she says.

The sister says, —I just want to know where they are being held. The soldier isn't listening because what she says has ceased to be of any relevance at all. He comes around the desk, grabs her arm and pulls her into a small room.

Chapter 21

When I open my eyes the house is dark. I lie perfectly still. After a minute my eyes recognise the vertical shape in front of them as one leg of the draftboard, and the horizontals beyond as the shelves, my shelves, in my map room. Everything is in its place. I sit up, cross-legged, under the draftboard. My sister's corner is darker than the centre of the room. I reach up and unhook the headlamp from where it hangs at an angle to the slope of the board. I aim it at the corner and squeeze it on. Empty. The house is quiet.

I get up and go through the rooms, flicking lights on, scanning the angles of each one. Her clothes and sleeping bag are gone from my bedroom, her shampoo from the edge of the bath. In the map room I crawl over the floor, checking for any changes occasioned by her presence. There is a slight scrape in the corner made by her easel on the first day, before I gave her the sheet. It can be accounted for with only minor adjustments. I feel immense relief as I turn off the lights. I drink my glass of water in the kitchen. As I replace the glass I know that it will not be displaced, as I close the cupboard I know it will not be reopened. The air is dry. She is gone.

There are three messages on my mobile from colleagues, which can be dealt with tomorrow. I work until midnight, ticking like a clock. Then squeeze off the headlamp, swing it onto its hook under the draftboard and go to bed. My sister's absence in the bedroom is like a blessing. Sleep comes uninterrupted in the silence. I dream of navigation. The sea is calm, the moon is full, the map under my hands is perfect. The dream map is of heightened relief, more real, more detailed than I can ever manage. It flips perception, it makes of scale a sleight of hand: sometimes it is continental, sometimes, at the blink of the eye, it is of shores, it is of grains of sand, more specific than is meaningful, more specific than I can bear.

The map makes a sound like a humming like a whine. I smooth its surface to calm it, I run the flat of my palms along the edges, I say —Shh. Then there is a shudder, a clunk, and the map drops down into the darkness, disappearing from my sight. My eyes flick open.

21.5

When the sister is hit or raped sometimes she flies away as if the force knocks her out of her own body, she gets knocked out and watches the soldiers hitting or raping someone else. Sometimes she can't manage it though, gets trapped in her body, feels like she's running through it looking for a way out, feels like she's tugging at something that won't let her go through all the pain and fear, or even that it's the pain and fear that has her that won't let her leave because it takes up so much space, needs all her attention. At first she just stuck to the cousin line, that they didn't know each other very well, had never been close, that they were travelling south together to leave, that she didn't know anything else, that she just wanted to know what happened to her and the child. Then she realises it doesn't matter what she says so she says nothing.

When they are not there she wonders if the circle drawn next to her lover's name means enemy, if it refers to ethnicity or perhaps politics. She wonders if the diagonal line through the boy's circle means relative of an enemy. Or child. Or dead. She wonders if a circle has been drawn next to her own name, and if there is a line. She thinks about these things while she's waiting in the dark, overnight in this locked room, the third night, she thinks, though it seems like so much longer. She listens for anything, everything, every sound pumping under her skin especially the jingling of keys which could mean they are coming back.

21.75

The place is dark when I open my eyes. I am sitting up in bed, shocked out of sleep. Listening to the knock on my apartment door, my breathing high in my throat. I thought it might be her but through the peephole I could see their uniforms and I opened the door like an idiot thinking they had made a mistake. I forgot that we were now living by the dice, by the sword, that the laws no longer mattered, were changing daily or being overruled. They could arrest me, and they could keep me, and they didn't need to tell anyone and I couldn't tell anyone. They didn't need a reason. They could get things wrong, but there was no way they made mistakes.

At the police station, still in my pyjamas, they asked me my name again and again as if it were evidence in and of itself. They asked for the name of my dead father, my missing mother, my sister, my cousins. They asked the names of my cousins again and again. They asked me my sister's name again and again as if it were a condemnation. They asked when I had last seen her, how often I saw her, and if I shared her political opinions. I said last summer, every now and then, and I don't even know what they are. They asked me my political opinions and I said I don't have any.

At first I was relieved that I was guiltless and did not have to dissimulate, did not have to keep anything from them, but as the hours passed I saw it didn't change anything. They asked if I had a connection to a certain radical group I had heard of but knew nothing about. They asked if I knew the names of people in the group, they kept saying one woman's name, watching my face, then punching it, then watching it, they kept saying names as if expecting some sort of reaction but I didn't know which.

The only escape is inwards and I have been doing it all my life. I can disappear. I can unravel the architecture of my mind, I can raze it to the ground until nothing is left but the blank slate. They kept asking the questions but I could no longer understand, could no longer comprehend the concept of a question, of speech. It didn't stop the pain but it stopped the logic of its origin, its cause was detached from the questions being asked so that there was no way to respond even if I wanted to, so that the concept of response was nonsense. My mother used to say it's like you're not there, flicking the tea towel in frustration. I think at one point I remembered that, and laughed.

Chapter 22

The house is dark when I open my eyes, I am sitting up in bed, shocked out of sleep. I touch the side of my leg to check I am awake, alive and in the present. Silence. Then the whining noise starts again. It is water in the pipes. The water is on somewhere, someone has turned on a tap in the house. It clunks off. My left hand flings back the covers, my right twists the lock of the window above my bed, they come together to push the pane upwards and I am out in a single breath. I run. I tear through the shrubs at the side of the house I leap the gate I am in the street, I am in front of my house, I grip the railings of the low fence and breathe. All the blinds are closed of course, there is no light visible at the windows' edges. The windows themselves are closed, the garden beds below them undisturbed. My bare feet are cold on the asphalt footpath, and stinging.

Has she left me open to this invasion, this attack, did she leave my house vulnerable in some unimagined way? Was there a lock I did not check, an opening, a rift she occasioned by her departure? I walk the length of the front fence, my hands gripping in measured intervals the painted metal of the railing, wet with dew. The street is silent. When I reach the far end of the fence I peer into the darkness at the other side of the house and think I see a movement at the blind-less kitchen window, a shadow darker than the surrounding night. I hitch up my nightshirt and climb the fence. The brittle grass scratches under my feet as I cross the garden and slide into the narrow space between the side wall and the fence. I edge along the wall, my palms to the bricks, and at the kitchen window I have to stand on tiptoe, my calf muscles cramping, to see in.

Nothing in the kitchen. Through its doorway I see the map room and the draftboard, still and empty within my angle of vision. Then a light goes on somewhere. It is further away—through the map room door the corridor is lit slantwise. From the way the light falls I know that it is the bedroom light which has been turned on at the other side of the house. I continue around to the backyard, noting the windows as I go, noting the lack of any sign of entry. I pause at the back door, squeeze the handle. It is unforced, locked, the bathroom window likewise. The presence in my house has arrived without leaving a trace. How can this have happened, how can there be water and lights going on in my hermetic house?

I continue to the final corner and press my back to the bricks, turning my head to peer around the other side of the house. I see the block of light that falls from my open bedroom window onto the bushes and the fence. Then a shadow moving, cast from within the bedroom. I bring my head back and push myself closer to the wall. I hold my breath, caught between fear and the need to know, my neck tense. I am thinking I will be brave, I will creep through the darkness to the window, I will confront this presence, when out of that same darkness comes a voice.

It says my name.

I turn my head around the corner. As if in a far mirror I see my sister's head turned out of the bedroom window. She says —What are you doing out there? I breathe out fear and breathe in anger. By the time I get to the window she has left the bedroom. I hear her in the corridor unlocking the front door, she calls me around. I push past her bristling, slam the door, bolt and chain it, go to the bedroom, bang the window closed, slide the lock back into place, check under the bed, the cupboards, back into the corridor, I sweep through the house turning on lights making sure that no invasion other than hers has occurred in the time I was out, with the bedroom window opening the house like a wound.

She follows, saying sorry, mumbling that she didn't mean to wake me and certainly not scare me. I scan the doors and windows from inside and can see no sign of entry. She is saying she just got so thirsty, saying something about a heater that dries the air. I spin around to face her. —You stole my key and made a copy, I say. She is indignant, says, —No.

—Then you were still here, hiding.

She doesn't respond, but there is something else in her face now. Guilt. —Where? I ask.

She sighs. —In the basement, she says.

And I cannot imagine what she hopes to achieve with such a claim, unless it is change the mood, throw me from my anger, unseat me so that she might regain some control of the conversation.

—I don't have a basement, I say, my tone measured. For a brief moment she looks confused, then she raises her eyebrows and makes a clicking sound with her tongue.

—Yes you do.

My fury notches upwards.

—I've been mapping this house for two years, I think I'd know if I had a basement.

—What do you want me to say?

I raise my arms and let them fall, wanting to laugh, wanting to hit something.

—Where then? I say. —Where does it start, where does it go down?

—The door in the corridor.

—Which door?

—The door that's not the lounge room, not the bedroom and not the bathroom. The other door.

—That's a cupboard, I say. —A storage cupboard for the owner.

—There was some stuff inside.

—The owner's stuff.

—It blocked the view of the stairs.

I feel like I'm falling, like the floor has plunged away by a matter of centimetres then slowed to an elevator-stop. She walks through to the corridor and opens the cupboard door.

—Look.

I haven't seen inside the cupboard since the rental inspection: the owner locked it in front of me, saying he needed the storage and had reduced the rent accordingly. I had nothing of my own to store in any case. Now my sister has pushed his boxes to one side, leaving a trail in the dust. She squeezes past and rummages on the wall behind them for a light switch. A bare bulb below eye level illuminates the first of the narrow, steep stairs which descend out of sight. I put my hand on her shoulder and press her back into the boxes so that I can see down. Nine visible steps then darkness. A warm damp smell.

The pitch of the steps makes me sick. I feel ashamed, incompetent. All the fury I had reserved for her for being present twists into an anger at myself for this absence of knowledge, this failure to comprehend. I turn to her.

—How did you know? I ask. —What were you doing in here?

—I was just curious. I wanted to know what was inside.

—But it was locked. How did you get in?

—Come and see it, she says, and starts down. I prickle with frustration that what's before my eyes, is before my eyes. Under my bare feet these ladder-steep stairs that shouldn't exist. There is no handrail; I steady myself against the wall as I go down. When we get to the bottom she says, —Locks are not really a problem.

There is electricity: a single light bulb in the centre of the ceiling, my map room floor. At first I estimate three point four deep by two point six wide, but at once I am unsure. The walls are closer together at the top and the corners are unfaithful: it is a frustum, pyramidal. The height is easier—I can do it relative to my sister as she moves forward, ducking, so only one point seven maximum. With my back straight I look up and have a good eight centimetres. She has the sheet I gave her laid out as a lining between her sleeping bag and the tiled floor. Her backpack is in the corner, next to it an oil heater. Crossing the walls are great hardwood beams which I realise are the foundations of my house.

It's hot. Even barefoot in my nightshirt I start to sweat under my arms; I feel it trickle down my side. I lean into the wall and am horrified by the friability of the plaster which dissolves into a sandy dust under my fingertips and behind my back. I hear the grains fall to the floor. The air is dry, there is not enough oxygen. A headache is coming from far away. The adjacent walls enter a slow slide like parallel rulers, they keep their relationship to each other but not to their corners, not to the planes above and below, not to me. The floor tiles are frozen in a wave as if burying something. My mother, I think, unreasonably, mournful. All the weight of the house seems to bear down upon the place. It is insupportable. It crumples me.

I feel the wall scraping upwards along my back and watch the wave of tiles roll towards me. I know this is low blood pressure, I know I will need to lie down before I fall down but I cannot lie here. —It's the shock, I say to my sister, but I can hear shouts in the street, blasting, explosions, gunfire pounding through the city above us. This is a shelter, a bunker, a grave, there are bones under the floor. No. Blood surges in my limbs. My sister has me under my arms. —No, I say to her, —this is a trap.

—Sit here. Put your head between your knees.

She places me on the first step and I look up, there are only nine steps after all, I am not so far down. I manage to stand up. I can find my way out: all I need is strength in my legs and here is the cupboard and here is my house; I feel blown up, staggering, wounded, I find my way to the map room and lay myself on the floor.

Outside my window I hear a group of people pass shouting, drunk. An early tram rumbling in the distance. I hear my sister climb the stairs after me and come into the room. She sits cross-legged on the floor beside my head and places her warm hand on my forehead. She says, —You don't have a temperature. I resist arguing the inefficacy of this method of temperature-taking. —Are you going to throw up? she asks.

—When did you buy the heater?

—What?

—It's too big for your backpack. You bought it when I was out.

—I bought it today.

—You don't have a key. You went out and left my house open. With me sleeping here.

—No.

—So you broke back in.

She says nothing.

—Is my house that easy to break into?

—No. It's very difficult. She sighs. —Are you okay now? Physically, I mean.

—Yes.

—Then I'm going back to bed.

—I want to talk to you about this. This basement.

—In the morning.

She gets up. I turn my head and watch her heels recede towards the cupboard. She closes the door behind her. She knows I won't dare follow her down there.

22.5

When the sister is hit or raped she runs through the cells of her mind looking for her twin who can reason a way through this, who will know how to analyse it, who will be aware of some principle that can help them both. The sister glimpses her twin raising walls, she sees her twin disappear behind them, she chases her twin through all these compartments she is creating, all these walls and doors, through what is becoming a maze with fewer and fewer exits, fewer and fewer alternatives, the sister keeps running and finally sees her twin, somewhere small, somewhere central, building up the last wall which will separate them, airtight, leaving no gaps, leaving no way in to her. The sister slaps her palms on the wall between them and shouts out her name, she spins around and the doors are no longer where she thought they were, she is disoriented, wonders if the floor is a wall and throws herself against it but it doesn't give because there is a rigidity to the structure which has hardened like new bone. The sister knows her twin is doing this for the sake of control, for the sake of sanity, but she feels abandoned, she feels trapped in the world while her twin has escaped.

Chapter 23

When I wake up I don't know my own house. We are estranged. The ceiling grins down on me in a victory of betrayal. God knows what it's hiding. I turn onto my side and shut my eyes, breathing in and out into my pillow, trying to find a rhythm, wondering if I can set the tempo, wondering if I have any control at all. I tell myself control is a simple matter of perception, of definition. I perceive three problems. I define them as the presence of my sister, the existence of the basement, and the failure of my mapping.

My eyes closed, I concentrate on sound. The neighbour's car pulling out of the driveway. Then nothing. A pause in the air. The house is between movements.

These gaps are dangerous. The mind needs something to consider, something to reach towards, or else it falls through. I am unsure of the passing of time. I hear my clock ticking but I have slipped back into sleep, into the war, all around me I can smell it and feel it on a new depth of scale, all closer, bigger than before. And there is no longer any such thing as getting up and going to work, there is no daily routine, there is no regular passing of time though the clock is ticking and you have to save yourself, you have to avoid the soldiers and bombs, you have to get the hell out of there. I have to walk away from the police station without looking back, I have to run on my bruised feet, my legs of sand carrying me, pumping me forward around the cars loaded high with everything their owners could carry, around the holes in the street, the exposed basements, my blue face blending in among all the broken people, making my way back to my apartment, clinging to the walls at the whirr of another bomb falling, all that stone, as we gripped it, sanding away our fingerprints.

I open my eyes, in time to see the minute hand flick to just before six. Then the second hand gliding a smooth circle around the face, wiping three six nine twelve. The clock clicks into alarm mode, I shoot my hand from under the covers and hit it on the head.

Back in my apartment I felt the absence of pain like a presence, a return to form, a sweetness in my body. I found myself grateful, simply grateful for my limbs and torso and head, I felt them heavy as gold. I sat in the dark of my apartment, my bags packed, door locked, lights out, listening to the bombings and the sirens and the shouting in the corridor, waiting for my sister, who was three days late. Holding on to my legs.

I was made to feel grateful for nothing at all. I know it's a psychological strategy that enables you to survive, especially in times of crisis. To expect nothing, to feel lucky just to have yourself. But it fades. You forget where your limits are, the borders of your own sphere of influence and control. You start expecting more from people, or, worse, from structures and processes which are indifferent to you. You forget that if they appear to support you it is only by chance and not design.

There is an almost imperceptible vibration in the air, an unfamiliar rumbling which increases in volume until it drums on the roof tiles like timpani. I sit up, keeping the covers pulled tight around me, and look out the window. Rain. Slicking the road in the pre-dawn darkness, running wet dust over the footpath, marbling the telegraph poles. I let the curtains fall and sit cross-legged on the bed with my back to the wall.

The last problem is the worst. The map is not a compromise, unfinished or symbolic; it is simply wrong. It is a map of a house without a basement, a house which doesn't exist because the basement does. The map is therefore a disaster of the form, founded in ignorance, showing no consciousness of the reality of the terrain it is attempting to cover. It is an illusion, a fable, a fiction posing as fact, an outrage. It will need to be destroyed.

I push the covers back and walk barefoot to the bathroom, grab the metal bin from under the sink, then to the kitchen for a box of matches from the drawer. Back in the map room the floorboards are cool under my feet. My mind takes some time to analyse what my eyes see on the draftboard. Or rather what they don't. My skin goosepimples. The bare wood is exposed, empty. There is a hole in its heart where the nail marking the Point of Beginning has been removed. The map is gone.

23.5

Tonight there are the close sounds of war: guns, grenades, screaming, shouting. In the deep of it the door is shouldered open and two soldiers fly into the room. When they regain balance one points a gun at the sister's head while the other scans the room. The sister stares at them from her corner. The one with the gun looks her up and down then speaks to her in her own language. Pseudo-soldiers then. He tells her to get out.

The sister stands with her back pushed into the doorframe and watches them continue down the corridor, kick in doors, fire into rooms, go further and further into this building which stinks of smoke and fear. In front of her is the room she walked into, of her own accord, three days earlier. Through the darkness and smoke she can still see the mangled pencil shavings in the ashtray on the counter. She bolts across the empty space to the tiny office behind the desk. The body of the pencil-soldier lies on the floor, cramped and folded into the diagonal. The sister steps over him, her foot slipping in the bloodied corner space left by his body, and grabs the register from the shelf.

She runs, as much as she can, back along the road she has started to know like home, this time with pain everywhere not just her knee. She has the register folded under her clothes where it keeps the wind from her stomach and chest. She comes back to the wooded place where her lover and the boy are gone. Her backpack is still hidden under the leaves and branches where she left it. She hauls it onto her shoulders and keeps going, wanting to put distance between her and where she was, as if safety were a matter of kilometres.

She has no map: it was in her lover's backpack. She pushes forward lost, with no idea where she has started or where she should aim to go. The next day she crouches in one of the out-buildings of an abandoned farm and searches the register for a key, a legend. Something that will tell her what the circle means, what the diagonal line. Nothing. It is a simple list of names and dates followed by symbols, some the same as her lover's and the boy's, some different. It's a code. If she knew something about their policies, about what happened, in per-centage terms, to the people they arrested, she might be able to break it. But she doesn't. She wonders if anybody does. She finds her own name in the register under the date of her enquiry. It too is followed by a circle cut by a diagonal line, like the boy's, and after that there is a number which she realises is the number preceding her lover's name on the register. She notices the boy has the same number after his circle and so she decides to assume the diagonal line means relative of the person whose number is suffixed. She realises there are other possibilities but decides to believe this one, the one she can live with, at least for as long as it's tenable.

She keeps the register. There is meaning in it, even if it's incomprehensible to her.

The next day she comes to the coast but feels too exposed, so stays a little inland where there are hiding places. At one point she climbs a hill high enough to see the horizon. Beyond it, to the south, is the city where her twin is waiting for her, if she is waiting. The planes and boats were still leaving when she last heard the radio, only five days ago, in her bedroom, with her lover. But the international organisations were pulling out and the evacuations of refugees would stop once they were gone. The sister considers her options. She decides she wants to live. She follows the coast south.

Chapter 24

The house is lit up with anger as I lift the bin above my head and bang it down against the floorboards with all my force. The walls rebound the clang of the bin as it tumbles on the boards, the sound waves rolling and crossing in the corridor, the kitchen, every corner of the house. —Bring it back, I shout. The sound echoes and fades into the dull roar of the rain.

For a senseless, blissful moment I imagine that my sister too is gone, even, briefly, that the basement was a dream. I look over my shoulder through the doorway to the corridor. Beyond it, the cupboard door is framed, smaller, like an exercise in perspective. The handle turns.

My sister appears, bleary and empty-handed. She shuffles over to the draftboard, glances at the bin still swinging in decreasing arcs on the floor. She picks up the matches and lets them drop back onto the draftboard. —That's what I thought, she says, going back towards the basement stairs.

—You have to do two things, I say. —You have to bring the map back up here and then you have to get out.

—I don't want to do either of those things, she says, and shuts the cupboard door behind her.

I drop to the floor to see if I can see through between the boards. Not much. I grab a pointed knife from the kitchen and use it to clean out the years of grime, sliding it along between the boards until I find a softness where the joining tongue has begun to rot. I stab at it with the knife to make a small gap I can look through. I can't see anything but flashes of movement. I should be above the corner where she has put her sleeping bag, and from the rustling I hear, she's getting back in.

—You said you'd leave, I say through the gap.

—No I didn't, she answers.

I pause. Didn't she?

—Well I said I wanted you to leave. And this is my house.

—Not the basement, she says.

—What?

—Not the basement. If you didn't know it was here it mustn't have been on the lease—you're not renting the basement.

—You're not serious.

—Not really. But it's a decent argument.

—No it's not. You can't live down there. There's nothing, no water, nothing.

—The kitchen pipes pass through. It would be easy enough to divert them. I could go to a hardware store. I know what to do.

—I don't want you here.

—I won't be there, I'll be down here.

—What about food? What about showers, the toilet? You will have to come up eventually.

—You'll have to go out eventually. You'll have to sleep eventually. That's when I'll come up. You need never see me. I won't even cross your path. How can that bother you?

I roll over and look at the draftboard above me. Light shines through the hole of the Point of Beginning like a celestial body.

—I want my map, I say at low volume, because I didn't expect to say it. There is a pause, and I assume she hasn't

119

heard. Then, —I'm looking after it, she says.

At work I tidy documents into parallel piles and arrange them in order of increasing urgency along my desk. I wonder if my sister is seriously putting us beyond negotiation, consciously taking this disagreement into the domain of power, of force? It is on my side: I have rights, there is the rule of law here, I am a legal tenant and the map is my property. I could go down there, take it from her hands, demand that she leave the house.

Does she think that I think that if I threw her out she could simply break back in? Does she think I can't go down there in the first place? Does she think I won't call the police because of what happened to us, does she think I think these police are the same as our police, does she think my fear makes me incapable of telling the difference?

I look up removal companies on the internet. I could ring the owner, explain that my sister has settled into a basement I didn't know existed, get a truck, find another place and leave no forwarding address.

But then I need to get the map back, or rather the map has to cease to exist. And that basement bothers me. Houses in this country don't have basements. Perhaps I'm going mad. Or my sister is. She's the one who found it.

I need to calm down. I search my desk for something that will settle my mind, something readable, something in two dimensions. I flick through the maps from the coastal project but they don't help, they are of places I have never been to and never will. I want to see a place that I understand, that I have created, that is mine. I want my map back.

Then I remember I have another one. I feel it against my skin. And suddenly I need to see it, to see my country once

120

more the way it was, to see if it matches the way I remember it to be. To check that it isn't similarly hiding things from me.

I pull the USB stick from under my clothes and push it into the computer port. The computer clicks through its processes and my files appear on the screen in front of me. But I can't open them. I search the program folders for the Global Map software and find it is security protected. The dialogue box with its irritating ding coming up instead, again and again, an exclamation mark in a triangle and the message: access denied.

—Hey.

I shut it down and look up. The mathematician is leaning through the doorway.

—I didn't know you were famous? she says.

I don't know what she's talking about. She says it like a question, but that could just be the way they speak.

—Sorry? I ask.

—I googled you, she says. —Came up with a couple of newspaper articles. Couldn't understand them, but it was your name and lots of photos of paintings. Are you a painter too?

I raise my eyebrows at her. —That's my sister, I say.

—Oh. It looked like your name.

They think all our names look the same. That's why they pronounce them so badly..

—No, I say.

She moves her head slightly as if she's going to argue the point, then seems to think better of it. She taps the doorframe once with her hand, gives a tight smile and leaves.

I take my computer keyboard by its sides and tap it rhythmically against the desk. I feel all over the place. I need to focus on one thing at a time. First I need to finish my report on shrinking states, or I could lose my job, which will mean losing the rent money, which will mean losing the house and everything it might or might not hold. I eject the USB stick, tuck it back into my clothes, and go to my final chapter— methodology, which I always do last, needing the retrospect. Then it comes to me. In attempting to explain why all previous heights above sea level are rendered obsolete with the rising waters, I am struck by its relevance to my own project. Is it not a simple question of level? Of which horizontal plane you take as zero, of where you set the upper and lower limits? And, in this case, of what you do with landscapes that float above and below the one you're mapping? Which in geographic cartography is admittedly rare.

The zero plane of my map hovers around the Point of Beginning, looking down into the negative of the floor, the walls and shelves rising into the positive. I haven't tried to take into account where other planes cut in and block the view. The ceiling has set the upper limit of the verticals and the floor the lower. The space between the ceiling and the roof, for example, is another missing landscape: that didn't make me question the map's validity, so why should the basement? There is, however, no reason not to add in these other levels, make of the map a sort of palimpsest. Or have several maps which overlay each other, on tracing paper, perhaps, and then permanently bound. It occurs to me that I've been too hasty in my judgement. The map isn't wrong, it's just partial. I mean, part of something bigger.

I need to get it back, and then add to it. I could go down to the basement and get it, simply take it from my sister. She would not, surely, fight over it. But I'm afraid. Not of her, of the basement. I reason this terror is simple fear of the unknown: once the irregularity of it has been accounted for, formalised, mapped, then I will be able to consider it just another room. I will be able to handle it.

I will need to find a way of mapping the basement without going down there. I will need a long thin strip of metal, and a chisel.

24.5

The sister stands on the landing outside her twin's apartment, sees the neighbour's door open a crack, feels the eyes of the elderly lady hiding in there. She knocks at her twin's door. There is no answer, the lights are out but she can hear breathing on the other side.

—It's me, she says.

The door opens. The sister looks down at her twin, small as a bird in the crack of light that comes through the landing window. Her face also bruised.

—You're late, her twin says.

—I'm sorry.

—I thought you were bringing someone.

—No.

The sister decides not to say anything about her lost lover, or the child. It's not that she wants to keep it a secret, it's just that if she tries to explain it, it will sound so much less important than it is. And then there is the feeling that she should have done more to find them, to save them. The guilt that she is still alive. One of the lucky ones.

24.75

When my sister finally arrived at the flat in the city where I lived, during the war, I couldn't bring myself to open the door. I stood there in the dark with my forehead pressed to the wood. I knew it wasn't the same knock as the police who had come two days earlier. There was a gentleness to it, a hesitancy. Still. My hand on the doorhandle I couldn't turn it. It was her voice that released me. She said, —It's me. And my hand moved because in her voice was all the surety of childhood, because her voice was familiar in every sense of the word.

As soon as I saw her I knew why she was late. Her face was bruised like my own. She squeezed past me with her backpack, just like she did when she arrived here, as if everything were normal, as if she were just my sister paying me a visit. I had thought she would be bringing someone but she said no. I didn't ask any more questions. I still haven't. It takes all my strength to discipline my own experience. I can't deal with hers as well.

She knows, however, because of our shared experience, that I would never again voluntarily walk into a police station. That no matter how much she is disrupting me, I would never put her into their hands.

Chapter 25

The house is lit up when I arrive home. It sits like a stranger in the dark, windows glowing from within. I approach it against instinct, hiding my hardware store purchases behind my back. The key sticks in the lock. I will assume, against my better judgement, that this is the result of the rain. The door itself resists, before opening with a jolt. I tilt the metal strip I've bought and slide it along the floor next to the skirting board. I shoulder the door back into its frame and drive the bolt home. Nothing moves. Even the insane parallelograms of the corridor seem temporarily subdued. The cupboard door is closed.

I pad through the rooms flicking off the lights. A contained glow streams upwards from the gap between the floorboards I made this morning. My sister must still be down there, with the light on. I stand with my back to the sink in the dark kitchen, drinking my glass of water and looking through the doorway. Next to the diffuse bar of light, the draftboard sits, naked without the map. Its dimensions seem reduced; it looks like just another piece of furniture. I wash and replace the glass, keeping one eye on the map room. Then take a deep breath and walk in there like I owned the place.

The map room is cold and silent. I drag the metal strip in from the corridor and lay it across the floorboards. I clip on my goggles, kneel down and prop myself on my elbows so that the strip is just centimetres from my eyes. I stretch up, take the headlamp from under the draftboard, clip it to my forehead and squeeze it on.

I flick my dividers into my right hand and with the sharp tip begin etching millimetres into the strip of metal, measuring from the base. I work from the outside in: I can't risk a slip at the measuring edge of what is to be my longest ruler. More than once the dividers flip up and scratch at my neck. It's rough, but it'll do for the first draft.

It takes all my will not to be distracted by the grain of the boards so close in the illumination of the headlamp, their Mandelbrot swirls which resist all measurement and so give me the urge to try. At one point my eyes slide over the gap I made between the boards and the sudden light from the basement through my goggles is blinding. I angle my headlamp in counterpoint to the upshining light, my eyes watering and blurring until I close them against the sting. Then I hear a swish and unclip my goggles to see below me a slip of paper, vertical, standing on nothing, its bottom corner between the gap. It rises up like an inspiration and falls sidewards. A note from my sister. I take it in the arms of my dividers. It says: How was your day?

25.5

When the sister walks out of the motel room she goes to the intersection where the trucks sit exuding fumes at the red light. She peers through the windscreens until she finds a woman in a hatchback who looks like a safe bet. She knocks on the passenger side window. The woman unwinds it and says hello. The sister struggles for the words to ask to be taken in to the city. The woman says she doesn't understand. The lights change and she drives off. The sister looks at the road signs, adjusts the straps on her backpack and starts walking.

She needs to be alone, and anonymous. She needs to have no one to talk to in the evenings because the only person she wants to talk to is gone. She feels that if she started trying to deal with everything that had happened it would take the rest of her life, all her time, blot everything else out. And she has other things she wants to do.

Her twin doesn't need her. Her twin, the sister thinks, would have no trouble getting a lift to town. She knows how to look respectable and trustworthy, she will be able to use her education, her language skills, her employability. She will be able to make herself at home.

25.75

When she left I knew it was a sacrifice I had to make. There was no alternative, it was about survival. She would keep me wanting something different from the place I was in, she would keep me expecting to feel at home. She would be constantly missing the life we had left behind, she would want her studio, her easel high in the house of rooms with the women planting vegetables. She would be torn to pieces with grief. I couldn't survive like that, with all that wanting.

I didn't consider everything she would take with her.

Chapter 26

When I finish, the house is lit up from below. It is late in the night, I have chiselled out the tongued joints between every third floorboard, and up from the basement push walls of light. I pull the metal strip into the south-east corner and lower it through the first gap until I feel it tap onto the tiles of the basement below. One point seven one three, at the top of the floorboards. I slide the strip along the gap, keeping the perpendicular with a plumb line tied to the top, which swings and taps against the metal as I move. I sound the depths and undulations of the basement floor, noting the figures every five centimetres. The crossbeams are an irritation, requiring me to withdraw the strip and reinsert, and creating gaps in the data below them. But it will have to do for what is, after all, only a draft.

Later I will need to make adjustments for the swell of my own floor compared to the flat invisible plane around the Point of Beginning. The work is time-consuming, but manageable. I inch across the floor as the hours slide by. In the silence between my movements I think I can hear her brushing paint across a canvas. It's more an idea than a sound, more an emotion than an idea, like the feeling of slipping. It catches in my stomach.

I prop my ruler in a corner and turn on the headlamp so I can look through the gaps without getting blinded. I crawl over the floor until I find her. She is moving around the centre of the basement, under my draftboard. The plane of my floor flies so low she must be forced to curl her spine, pull her head between her shoulders to stay upright. From the quick, sweeping quality of movement I can only catch in glimpses, she is in fact painting, although I don't know on what. I look around me for her note, which lies unanswered nearby, between the bars of light. On its reverse side I write: Could you move everything to the north side of the room please? and pass it through the gap near where I last caught her movement. I feel it plucked down from my fingertips, and when it slips back up a second later she has painted a response over my words. It says: No. In magenta.

I suppose that was predictable. I fold the paper inwards so the paint can stain only itself. I try to think of ways I could get the upper hand. But I don't know what she fears. I don't know what she wants. I don't even know why she is still here.

I smooth out a fresh sheet of paper on the bare draftboard and begin to translate the first of the basement measurements into contours. As for her mess, if she won't shift it I will just have to map it as part of the landscape. I pass my ruler over the ridges of her sleeping bag and backpack, the sudden outcrop of the heater. Through the process I discover a table, or some other form of raised, rectangular construction, in the centre of the room. I assume that this is where she is painting, with paper or canvas laid out on top, but when I check the tip of my ruler it always comes up clean. Perhaps she is moving her work from the path of my measuring. A small blessing, I suppose.

It still takes three hours to do a rough draft. The finished product lacks the intricacy of my stolen map but it allows me to go to bed feeling safe. I roll it up and take it with me.

In sleep I am floating above her on my planks. I am a creaking to her, to me she is a termite, I dream the fear that she will destabilise me, that my house will fall, that my map will mean nothing. I dream grief at the thought of the fear being realised and start crying. The water that pours from my eyes runs in rivulets over the floorboards and drips through the gaps that I have created, streaking her painting until she shouts up, —Just set a scale and stick to it. I shout down, —Do you think that's the limit of my problems? Do you have any idea how far they extend? But her irritation gives me an idea. I get a bucket and a mop and wash the floor in sloppy seas of water. It drips through the gaps, tracking everything like a thousand snails. I think, smiling, that I've found what she fears and I'm right because she shouts up, —You're ruining my painting. I say, —You're annihilating the very foundations of my mapping, and it's true because as I say it we hear a great crack as the heat she has brought to the basement gets into the supporting beams. One side of the house has just dropped by millimetres, taking with it the floor, the draftboard and the Point of Beginning.

Under the covers I pull the draft of the basement closer to my chest. Tomorrow I will go down there.

26.5

The sister wakes up, pulls herself out of her sleeping bag and stands. She paints, on the floor of the basement, a circle. The walls of the basement, which are the foundations of the house, touch the circle in four places like tangents. The sister feels that the circle is a hole, an absence that might swallow the house and all who sail in her. The sister feels that it is a clue, but needs another clue to decipher it. She pulls the prison register from her backpack and flicks again through its pages. It makes meaning but she doesn't know how to read it. She looks at the tiles of the basement. What she needs is a Rosetta.

Chapter 27

The house is breathing when I wake up, the bedroom walls opening and closing like bellows. My grip on the draft of the basement has tightened in the night, twisting the roll into my stomach and chest which rises and falls with my respiration. I become aware that there is music playing; a symphony pushing up from the basement; slipping in through the air vents and under the door. Its rhythm expands and contracts the space.

I hold the draft map scrolled to me as I go down the stairs. The music is in a march; I resist stepping to its beat. I stay low, even though there is no need—I keep my head pulled into my shoulders like when you hear the whistle of a bomb about to fall somewhere else. I don't look into the basement as I reach the bottom, I keep my eyes down and with an effort of will release my grasp of the draft map and unscroll it so that I can hold it between me and the room. It blocks the view of my sister, and is framed by the four planes reaching forward towards me, the walls, the floor of this place and my own floor above.

The map in front of my eyes gives me an indication of what lies beyond. It prepares me. I will not be surprised, like last time. I will not feel the loss of blood to my head, I will be able to follow its contours and guide the oxygen to my brain. I concentrate on my breathing. The smell of paint fumes is nauseating, it cuts into my throat and lungs. I feel low, below the world. The music is becoming more complex, higher-pitched. It is in a slow movement, one of the Romantics whom my sister likes so much.

When I feel ready I lower the draft map so that I can see beyond. My sister is looking at me from behind a table I now see is constructed from a scrap of plywood, propped on the owner's boxes. Across it is a thick piece of paper on which she is painting. She walks over to a portable CD player on the floor and turns off the music, the sense of urgency it created dropping away.

—Sorry, she says. —Did I wake you?

With the music off and the map in hand I feel reasonably calm. I scan the topography of the floor and my sister's possessions, comparing it all to my draft. Considering the circumstances in which it was made, I haven't done too badly. The room makes a lot more sense than it did last time.

—Where did you get that? I ask, nodding at the CD player. It's one of two things that weren't here when I mapped the area the night before.

—It was in one of those boxes at the top of the stairs.

—The owner's boxes? You stole it out of one of the owner's boxes?

—I didn't steal it, I just moved it. I mean, he's obviously not using it.

That's the influence of communal living for you. The other thing I've missed in the draft is a cheap tap which my sister has fitted into a pipe running from under the kitchen floor. It sits below a block of three floorboards, in a blank spot between the lines of my measurement. She has hung a small bucket from it, with brushes sticking out.

Then I see the walls themselves. I had assumed they were

135

featureless when making the draft: another error. On the back wall under the tap my sister has pinned her paintings to the beams, so that they hang away from the inward slope of the wall like washing on a line. They continue around to the left, along the north wall, the nearest only about a metre from where I stand at the bottom of the stairs.

But that's not all. I look to my right and see that covering the entire south wall are sheets of paper, pinned to the wall at their overlapping corners. Even from this distance I can see they are covered with lists of names and symbols, arrows between them with notes written in my sister's hand. With the draft map held open I step closer, my feet comfortable on the known unevenness of the tiles. I can just make out the writing in the dim light. Familiar names, from home. The edges of some sheets of paper are frayed along one side, the writing in original pencil, as if torn from a book. Others are photocopies.

—What is this? I ask.

She empties the cup of dirty water into the bucket hanging under the tap. —I was looking for someone, she says. —Still am, sort of.

That doesn't answer my question, but I notice two names are highlighted again and again.

—Look. My sister comes over, wiping her hands on a rag. She points to another name, unhighlighted, but underlined in pen. —That's how I found our aunt and her children, she says.

My aunt's name, in rough pencil. From it stretch three arrows in pen, ending at the names of my cousins on another page. Two crossed out, followed by hollow circles with lines through them. The other followed by a filled-in circle. It shocks me, to see these names, here. Not so much because of the time that has passed since I last thought of these people, but because they seem to belong to another world, which I no longer inhabit.

—But what is it? I ask again. —Where are these pages from?

—From the prisons, the military detention centres. It's a code. The circles mean that person is on a list. Political dissidents or just, you know, 'undesirable'. A diagonal line through a circle means relative of one of those people. When the name is crossed out that means they've been let go. Or escaped. When the circle's filled in that means they've been executed. I've checked it with the war crimes people—that's what it means.

I remember her emailing me, but I'd put it out of my mind. I touch the filled-in circle next to my cousin's name, then follow the arrow backwards to my aunt's name, draw my finger along and see it too is followed by a filled circle. Here is the evidence behind the email. Aunt and cousin dead, other two cousins presumably safe in exile.

I feel like I'm dipping slowly, up and down, like a boat in swell, the horror of it underneath me like a wave. The fact that even this was recorded, that it was given symbols and signs. It must have helped them to think of it as something reasonable, normal, like any other job, where records need to be kept, notes taken. The draft map has scrolled itself up against my leg. My right hand follows the list down from my aunt. They are magnetic, these names, in their syllables, the arrangement of consonants, the way they sound like my mother tongue. They draw the eye along like a magnet under iron filings. I scan through them for more relatives, and am stopped short. The air held in my mouth. My own name.

No. I breathe out. —My sister's.

I remember her bruised face when she arrived at my flat. It makes sense, that she would have been on one of these registers too.

—Your name, I say.

She is close to me, and looks at me rather than where I'm pointing. But I can't take my eyes off this name, written in someone else's hand, a guard, a torturer perhaps, a murderer. I follow it along to the symbol at the end.

—With a circle and a line, I say.

I feel trapped between the name and her gaze, I can barely move my lips to speak.

—Which of our relatives was a dissident?—I finally manage to ask—Did they mean our aunt?

—No, says my sister, —that was later. She drops her stare. I feel released, but keep my eyes on the name. In my peripheral vision I see her reach her own hand to the wall, and press the tacks that fix the sheets further into the beams and the soft plaster of the wall, as if she feared they would come loose.

—So who then?

—No one, she says. —No one you knew. I lied. I was looking for someone.

—What do you mean?

—I told them I was related to her.

I don't make the connection straight away, between what my sister has said and what happened afterwards, to me. So mesmerised is my mind by this name above my finger tip. It is so nearly my own name; it almost undoes me. Then it comes to me, not so much a revelation as an idea.

—We share relatives.

My sister looks at me again, and this time I pull my eye from the wall to meet hers. After a minute she sighs. —Yes, she says.

—So they thought your relative would be my relative too. She looks almost frustrated with me.

—Yes.

It becomes clear to me then, why they came to my house. Why they chose me. They don't make mistakes. But I'm not angry at my sister, she couldn't have predicted that. I don't blame her, not for this.

—Who were you looking for? I ask.

—Someone I loved. A woman. And her son.

The highlighted names. I look back at them, at first listed together, then at later dates separately. The latest date has the names still uncrossed, circles unfilled. Not definitively let go, then, not definitively killed.

—Is this what you haven't been telling me? I ask her.

—What are you talking about?

—You've been keeping things from me—is this it?

—Oh, you're kidding me. She stops pressing in the tacks and takes a couple of quick steps back to the table.

—Why didn't you talk about this? Why didn't you tell me what happened?

—You know what happened.

—To you, I mean.

—It's the same thing as happened to you.

She looks at me as if daring me to continue. To contradict her, elaborate, or in some way take this line of conversation to its logical conclusion. Instead I change tack.

—Can't you find where they last were held, at least? I ask, pointing at the pages with the last recordings of the highlighted names. —Can't you find out where they were taken from there?

My sister looks at me and lets her arms rise and fall to her sides. When I don't react she comes back over to the wall and examines it as if for the first time.

—No. That's the problem with all this. It gives us information on who was taken, why, and for how long. But it doesn't tell us where. There are no place names in the registers, and the camp locations were secret. I know vaguely where I was held, so we know the region at least for this one. She puts her hand to the section covered with the original register paper. And for some of these—she continues, pointing to certain photocopied sections—there are vague locations too, from other prisoners. But for this one—she puts her hand to the final entry for the two highlighted names—we have no idea.

—Who's 'we'? I ask.

—Oh, you know, the war crimes people. And that other UN thing that helps you find people, the ones that do the databases.

I've had no contact with any of them since my sister left. She lets her hands drop from the wall. She looks tired. I feel I should say some words of comfort to her, but what comfort can there be? Besides, it's too late for that. And she didn't even want me to know.

I look up and see the morning light from my map room barring the boards of the ceiling, my floor. The trickle of names remains on my mind's eye, between me and the boards. My sister's, particularly. Again and again.

—If you're here now, why wasn't your name crossed out? I ask.

She turns away from me and walks back to her easel in the middle of the room.

—I took the book with me when I escaped, she says.

I breathe in and out, my ribcage expanding, contracting. The papered walls rustle on my exhalations.

—Anything else? I ask her, my eyes still on the ceiling.

—No.

I hear her step over to the tap to refill her cup, shuffle back, squirt paint from a tube. She is used to this, I realise, to being surrounded by the handwriting of torturers. I have simply distracted her.

I can't even turn around. I stare at the light through my floorboards, unable to believe that my world is still up there, the world that I had just begun to know, to map. My neck muscles cramp. I am forced to drop my head and am again confronted by the full chaos of these letters and symbols. And numbers. I suddenly see the numbers, I don't know why I didn't notice them before. Figures before each name, consecutive within each section of the register, and then after some of the names, different figures.

—What are the numbers? I ask, looking over my shoulder at my sister.

She answers matter-of-factly, without looking up from the plastic plate where she has started mixing colours.

—The first is the number they give the prisoners as they come in, the second is for those who are relatives of dissidents. It refers back, or forwards, to the person they're related to, if and when that person is captured.

I look back at the lists and compare the numbers following my aunt and cousins' names. It makes sense.

—What about these other numbers?

—What other numbers? She glances over.

I point to them, where they head each page, in the top left or right hand corner, depending on which side of the original book the paper came from. They look familiar. Two capital letters followed by three numerical figures, then a dash and another three figures.

—Oh, she says, —we don't really know. Probably the reference code they gave the camp.

As she speaks I look at the number above my fingernail. It rises in me, this sense of knowledge, this feeling that I know—that I used to know—what this number meant.

—Or maybe the level of detention, my sister continues. —You can see the numbers change for different sections, you know, where they come from different prison registers.

No, that's not it. I can see the room where I knew what these numbers meant. I can see its pale green walls, the shelves and folders, labelled in my own language. I can see the computer screen where the numbers would come up day after day. In my office before the war. I remember now. I check the different numbers heading different swathes of paper. They all match up. It's been years since I've seen them, but I know what these numbers are.

I can feel my blood pressure dropping: my head getting lighter, my feet heavier, my sphere of vision closing in. I need to lean against something. Not the walls. I open out the draft map but it doesn't steady me. I need to hold on to something which touches the ground. I step towards my sister's table and feel the wall follow me, the heat of it against my back. I spin around and it is closer than I thought, the whole wall swinging in a continuation of my movement, the numbers there in the corners, in the corner of every page, inhabiting every single one. Two capital letters, three figures, a dash and another three figures. They swing out with the wall, reach the height of their arc, and fall back into place. I feel sick, sick with it to the soles of my feet, my legs weak with it. I look around to my sister and she hasn't looked up, our last conversation already forgotten. She is peering at her canvas, with her naked eyes.

I say her name.

She looks up at me. I grip the corner of her table with my left hand. I don't want to faint. I have to tell her first, in case I black out, in case I then forget.

—They're locations, I say.

—What?

—The numbers, in the corners. They're geographical co-ordinates.

She gives a short laugh.

—No they're not, she smiles at me. Don't worry, that did get considered. But then the format didn't match any maps, apparently, including the military ones.

I shake my head. My vision slides with each turn of my head, unsteadies me. The table sways under my hand.

—It's a very particular grid reference. There wasn't, there still isn't, any public information about it. Only about ten people knew it. Those working on the Global Map.

My sister puts down her brush and plastic plate. She doesn't have to look at me like that.

—Were you one of them? she asks.

—Yes.

I don't know how they got these coordinates, the military. I don't know why they chose to use them. Perhaps the smallness of the team working on the project made it the most secret system available. Perhaps someone who worked for me was involved. Perhaps the map served them in more ways than one. I need to lie down. I hang from the table with my left hand and stretch my right hand down to the floor. The tiles are cold and greasy under my palms, and then against my skin through my nightshirt as I lie on my back. My sister comes around to the side of the easel, and looks down on me.

—I feel dizzy, I explain.

She folds her arms and looks at me like our mother. Horizontal I feel the blood pushing into my brain; my vision expands outwards again, steadies, the nausea fades.

—Look, I say to my sister, taking one of the pieces of charcoal scattered on the floor and rolling on to my left side. I reach out my right hand and draw a rough outline of the borders of our country, as we last knew them, over the tiles.

—This is the area being mapped, I explain.

My sister shifts around the easel to see better and shuffles her weight from foot to foot, impatient.

—What do you mean? she asks.

—The country. You put a grid over it like these tiles.

I indicate the joints of the tiles as the lines of the grid. I look up at my sister. She gives a single nod.

—Each grid has a letter, I continue, marking them up. Then you divide up each grid again.

I hatch out a new grid five by five on the tile closest to me.

—Then each one of those has its own letter, that is, a combination of the first letter and a new letter. You can keep going, but we just used a two-letter reference.

144

I go over the lines I've marked with the charcoal, trying to get them straight.

—What are the six numbers? asks my sister.

—Eastings and northings.

—What are they?

—It's the distance east and north, respectively, from the south-west corner of that grid.

—And that gives the exact place?

I roll back and look up at her. —More or less, I say. —In this case within about a hundred square metres.

My sister turns away and goes over to the wall. She puts her hand on the sheet which has the last registered entry for one of the highlighted names. —Are you saying you were the only ones to use this system? she asks.

—Yes. Well, no, it's a well-established system of projection, but the original geodetic datum was new.

My sister frowns.

—Where we decided to put the grids, I explain. She's still frowning. —Imagine this grid is on tracing paper, I say, putting my palm to the charcoaled squares on the floor. —I can move it anywhere I want over the polygon. I can even make the squares bigger or smaller. You need to know how that's been done before you can find the coordinates. Do you see? That's why your agencies thought the numbers, or rather the letters, didn't match any existing maps—because they wouldn't have. They only matched the map that we were creating.

—But how do you know these are yours?

—I recognise them. When we did the projections, we wrote the coordinates in that specific way, to distinguish them.

—So you know where this is? She points to the number in

the corner of the page under her hand. She spells out the reference, louder than is necessary.

—The letters indicate north-east, I say, —but I can't remember for the figures. I'd need to check them against the map.

—You're telling me we can just get a map and find out where this is?

I roll my head against the floor. —No, I say. —That's what I've been telling you. It can't be just any map. These references are specific to the Global Map.

She drops her hand to her side in frustration and looks at me. I feel as if I were guilty of something, as if it were my guilt that failed to make these connections in time, that kept us both from seeing what was right in front of her face.

—Well where is this Global Map? she finally asks.

It was just chance, just a chance lack of knowledge, or rather the lack of us sharing the knowledge that we each had, by chance, inside our skins. She can't blame me for that. But I can't meet her gaze. I put hands over my face and close my eyes.

Part Three

CHAOS

Chapter 28

When I open my eyes the house is lit up. It shines through my fingers, and when I take my hands from my face I see the floorboards above me slit with the sunlight pushing though from the map room. It grids the basement floor, capturing me, my sister, and everything she owns. The planes of the house creak against each other, stacked up over us like cards. I try not to breathe. My sister is standing above me, swaying, or else it's the floor that's swaying or else it's me, an illusion, all in my head.

My nightshirt is creased up underneath me, the tiles send a chill through the skin of my back. It seeps up through my ribs. I feel my heart beat against it, panicked, feel it surfacing as if for air, moving upwards away from the chill. I feel it beat against my sternum, trembling the buttons of my nightshirt, and underneath them, the memory stick which jumps between my ribcage and the fabric like something trapped.

I can't stay here. I push myself to my feet and stumble to the stairs, crawl up with the help of my hands against the stone, push past the boxes, the narrow cupboard door, into the light of my house, the map room, bright in the morning sun. I take the freshness of its air into my lungs, feel the oxygen circulating, normalising my system, stabilising me. Up here everything is in its place. There is no need for me to panic like that. I go through to the kitchen and wash the slime of the basement from my hands, dry them on the tea towel, fold it back over the oven door.

When I turn around my sister is there, leaning against the fridge. I breathe in, ready, but she doesn't move. She just stands there as if waiting for me to say something or do something, for her. I have to turn sideways to get through the kitchen doorway without touching her, I slide around the corner of the doorframe into the map room and have a clear run to the corridor. She follows me, silently, like a shadow three seconds late. When I get to my bedroom I turn around to face her, hold up my hand, close the door in her face and lock it from inside.

She thinks she holds all the cards. That is, she simply assumes that I will help. She is counting on our sisterhood, she is imagining that I think that by helping her I will help myself but I have no reason to believe that this is true. As I get dressed I feel fragile, almost like I want to be comforted by her but she is the source of my discomfort so I stay strong. I decide to keep a fixed distance because I would be all right if she weren't here bringing all this down on me. I just need to come to terms with this new situation.

'Come to terms with.' The phrase I learned from some well-meaning human services worker when I first arrived—something about coming to terms with the past, with the loss. I hadn't heard it before and the choice of words was revelatory. A phrase of military origin, surely, implying, it seemed to me, some negotiating power. —But tell me, I asked the social worker, —What terms should I be proposing to the past? What have I got to offer, or to threaten? My only options are surrender or flight.

Not so now.

I open the bedroom door and she is no longer there. But when I go through the corridor to the map room I see her on the other side, in the kitchen doorway, drinking a glass of water.

I lean against the doorframe of the corridor and look over the draftboard at her, not wanting to go in, not wanting to decrease the distance between us. She washes the glass, dries it, replaces it, then leans against the kitchen doorframe in a mirror of my own stance.

I refuse to meet her eye. I look around the map room, taking in its detail, noting how the alignment of objects has been maintained despite all the changes she has engendered below. Everything is in its place. Except the one thing, of course, clearly not where it should be. The draftboard is pitched perfectly to the sun like a solar panel, brilliant and empty. I realise I didn't see the map when I was in the basement. She still has it, hidden somewhere.

The only thing I need to come to terms with is her.

I look up. She is still looking at me, waiting.

—A map for a map, I say.

—What do you mean?

—The Global Map for my map. You give my map back to me.

She breathes out through her nose, purses her lips, tilts her chin to one side. I can hear the clock ticking in the bedroom behind me. Finally she says, —Okay.

—I'll need the coordinates, I say, stepping towards the window so that she can pass. She moves through the map room and corridor in a few steps. The handle of the cupboard door flicks back into place as she lets it go from the other side.

I wait a few minutes, listening to her rummaging for a pencil below. The widened gaps between the floorboards make me uneasy, they make the room seem perforated. But they are useful, I tell myself, they enable me to see through to the other side. I lay myself down with my head near the south wall, close my left eye and put my right to the gap. I see the top of her head and her hands; she is standing by the wall, writing down the figures. When she is finished she looks up at me. I pull my head back and she pushes a folded edge of newspaper up through a gap. I take it, glance at the figures, refold it and put it in my pocket.

—I might need a few days, I tell her.

There was controversy, about the way we did the grids. All the existing geological surveys covering the landmass that is, was, my country, had used their own geodetic systems, and so their own different grid references. At first we thought we'd just have to choose one, the most comprehensive one, and adjust all the other surveyed areas to that system to create a single standardised map. But there were politics involved. The particular landmass I call my country had changed hands a lot over recent history, its shape, and size. The different systems were the result of different administrations, working independently.

If I had chosen to work with one particular system instead of the others, for such an important national and international project, it would have been seen as a political preference, it would have opened up old divisions. So despite the extra work involved, and the impact on my budget and timelines, I decided we'd create a new one. It meant recalculating from all the old surveys, redoing some of the mapping itself, but in a way that enabled us to more comprehensively correct past errors, and to improve the quality of the work. Maybe that's why it was of use to the military.

Chapter 29

The house is lit up in my mind. I feel that I have to keep remembering it until I can get the map back, so I picture them one by one, all the rooms of my house on all their levels dividing and subdividing in the light of my looking. I will not allow the tram to take me away from it; in its rocking I imagine myself safe in the most central room of my house, in my map of the map room, scaled smaller than a draftboard, the blank square illuminated.

As the lift doors close I wonder how small a room can be tolerated, if my colleagues around me can only cope with this confinement because they believe it to be temporary. I imagine their panic if we were to be trapped in here, they would feel a sudden, intolerable sense of enclosure and yet they accept it as a means to an end, day in and day out. I don't need to accept it, of course. I live with it.

But this is getting bigger now. I will have to expand my focus. I will need to go out in space and back in time. I will need to consider the contours of my country beyond the four walls that have been enclosing me. I will need to think of myself as of the world.

I try to think of a story to tell the mathematician. I know she is providing advice for the Global Map project here—she would have access to the software. I wonder what story she would be sympathetic to. Apart from the truth.

In her office I sit opposite her desk, trying to shut out the noise of the figures on the print outs around her. She looks back at me, waiting. Finally she says, —You're not still trying are you?

—What? I ask.

—The Zeno thing. The infinite measuring.

—No. I'm doing it differently.

She smiles.

—Sounds wise.

Her phone rings. She picks up the receiver by a centimetre, replaces it, then takes it off the hook. Then she leans back in her chair, crosses her legs and looks at me.

They always look so honest here, so naïve, as if they don't expect you to lie to them. As if they don't see why you would. It makes me want to be worthy of trust, for her sake, but that may not be practical.

I reach under my collar and hook my finger around the strip of fabric that holds the memory stick. I draw it out of my shirt, pull it over my head and hold it forward to her, its metallic surface shining in my right palm. The strip of fabric curls and falls between my fingers. She looks from my eyes to my palm and back again.

—What's on it? she asks.

I don't know where to start. She hesitates, then leans forward and takes it between her thumb and forefinger. Her fingertips barely graze the skin of my palm, the strip of fabric ripples through my fingers and is gone.

It's all gone. She has it in her hand. I feel raw, as if I have lost the upper layer of my skin and am sensitive to her every displacement of air. With her thumb she pushes back the hinged cover of the memory stick and slides the exposed metallic tip into the USB port of her computer. She looks over at me. —What is it? she asks again.

I close my own hand and put it in my pocket, draw out the folded strip of newspaper and smooth it on my lap. The co-ordinates are listed in pencil, in my sister's clumsy hand. There are points where the pencil has gone through the paper as she wrote, without a surface to lean against, next to the wall. I look up. The mathematician is looking at the screen. —Can I open these files? she asks.

I want to say no, I want to grab back the memory stick and leave. I fear, unreasonably, that in clicking the mouse she will open me up, that I will be exposed. But I'm not guilty of any-thing. I have the right to have a map of my country, to carry it with me, I have the right to keep it to myself. This is my data more than anyone's. I made it. She turns back to me. —Is that what you want? she asks.

I swivel the chair one way and the other in a tight rhythm. What choice do I have anyway, if I want my map back?

I nod.

I hear her double click, pause, double click again. She frowns at the screen. —What language is this? she asks.

—Mine, I say.

She glances up, then looks back at the files. I watch her clicking and sliding and clicking the mouse as she moves through the files. I'm going to have to explain. She's not going to know what to look for. Then she says, —Where did these come from? They look like Global Map files.

I remember then, that there is the same way of organising the files in the different countries. One raster and four vector

155

application formats in the first folder, then once you open them up the same layout for each. The final folders labelled with a single letter. The whole project is, after all, about international consistency. She stops clicking and looks up at me.

—How did you get this data? she asks.

—It's mine.

—What country is it for?

—Mine.

She leans back again, folds her arms and tilts her head at me. —I thought it was all lost, she says.

I laugh. As if it were something funny, but not very important.

—So did I, I lie.

She doesn't move. She smiles, slightly, but only because I'm smiling. When I stop so does she.

I decide to tell her. Most of it, not all of it. I omit things, like my sister, and I add others, like the bit where I thought I'd lost the USB stick, where it had slipped into the lining of my suitcase and only fell out when I was trying to put the case on top of my wardrobe because I had to tilt it to get it up there and luckily I had forgotten to zip the case closed because otherwise the stick wouldn't have slid out, it would have stayed in there and I might not have found it for another two years.

It's details like that which make a story sound convincing. So I've heard. But she just stares at me across the desk.

—Why did you bring it to me?

—Because I can't access the software. I can't open the files.

—What's that? she asks, nodding at the strip of newspaper in my lap.

—The reason I need to.

The door swings open almost silently; it startles us both. I notice the mathematician reach forward and turn off the monitor in a subtle movement, as if adjusting the screen. I put the newspaper back in my pocket. It's one of her colleagues, a little out of breath. —God, he says, I've been trying to call. He notices me and gives a quick smile. —They've already started, he says to the mathematician.

—Shit, she says and starts pulling together documents. She glances up at me. —I've got a presentation, she says.

—I'll go set it up, says her colleague, already out the door.

I am worried that she'll forget the memory stick in her rush, or worse, pull it out of the machine without closing it properly, possibly corrupting the data. I stand up.

—No, she says, her voice low, indicating to me to stay where I am. She swings one arm into her jacket and grabs a pile of papers with the other as she heads out. She stops in the doorway and nods towards the computer. —It's all yours, she says, and closes the door behind her.

Chapter 30

When I arrive home the house is lit up. I can see that nothing has been disturbed. There are no footprints but mine on the path; through the window next to the door I can see everything is in its place. The clear surfaces, the swept fireplace, the maps tucked in their row of folders. The usual. First the security door, then the inner door. Once inside, the chain and bolt. I march through the rooms, flicking off the lights. I close the blinds in the map room, the curtains in the bedroom, shut the bathroom door. The house darkens, the twilight long gone. I am late home. My sister is nowhere to be seen. I drink my glass of water in the kitchen, wash it, dry it, replace it. Fold the tea towel back over the oven door. I am close now, I feel it. I am on the brink of control.

I move through the dark of my house without touching the sides. I swing my hand under the draftboard as I pass, feel the thump of the headlamp in my palm, unhook it, slide it over my forehead and flick the switch. It illuminates my workbag where I have left it, on the shelves; the circle of light tightening as I approach. I reach inside and pull out the small stack of A4 paper I have printed off. I lay out the sheets in order on the draftboard, easily, quickly, like a child's jigsaw. The Global Map of my country, in fragments. I line up the contours, aligning mountain ranges and coastlines, rejoining major roads and regional boundaries, the latter now largely obsolete. I tape it all together.

I hold on to the ridge of wood at the bottom of the draft-board. Here is my country, although it no longer exists like this. Here is my country, as it is in my mind, in my data and on my map. The last of its kind.

I take a blue pin and mark the location of my city apartment. With a green pin I mark the exact location, learned only a few hours ago, of where my sister was held. A red pin for her lover, a yellow for the child. They were all there at the same time, briefly, though my sister couldn't know that. Then the lover and child were moved on. With new red and yellow pins I mark their next locations. They were separated, the lover was moved north, the child south. Moved one last time, the lover.

I write the coordinates of each place on tiny slips of paper and mark the dates of imprisonment. Above it a number: one through four, to show the order of movement. The slips of paper are no wider than a strip of sticky tape, which I now lay over them, then extend to double the length. I curl the tape around the appropriate pin heads and along the backs of the paper strips, pressing the layers between my finger and thumb to make tiny, laminated flags. Afterwards I roll each strip in towards the pin in a tight scroll, so that they can be opened and closed at will.

I read the names of the towns surrounding the various places of detention. They are mostly in regions I have never seen, only passed through on the way to my mother's or sister's places. Regions we sketched in different colours in our school notebooks, regions which, in my mind, remain associated with certain festivals, historical events or ways of making bread. Since then they have, of course, become internationally known. The very names of the towns almost symbolic, in the world's common mind, with the war itself, evoking all those before-and-after images of destroyed architecture, of soldiers separating women and men at gunpoint, of that one reporter yelling, crying, inarticulate among the bodies. The names of the towns surrounding the lover's last holding place are the most notorious of all, for the massacres, the rapes, and the stories told about the camps nearby.

I straighten up and pull my coat tight around me. Here is the map my sister wanted, a map of the past, a map of all the worst things that had happened to her and the people she loved. Now that I have finished working on it I can't even look at it. I turn away and walk around the room, trying to get the chill of it off me.

I wonder who did this. I draw up the faces of my colleagues from the well of my memory and wonder which of them gave these grid references to the military. I wonder what else they gave away. I wonder how much of what I thought was mine has actually been used, secretly, against me. And my sister. My colleagues' faces blur together in my mind. I would never have thought to ask them about their politics. I never would have thought that, being scientists, they were capable of the irrationality, the partiality of it all. The hate.

I stop side-on in front of the draftboard and look again at the map over my shoulder. I have not marked the place my sister came from, the house of rooms. I have never known its coordinates, not seeking to map it, and now find I can no longer remember which town it was closest to, which hill or lake. I can no longer imagine where it might lie among these crinkles and swirls; all I can see from this map is my interpretation of what happened afterwards. That the child was moved south to be adopted out. That the lover was moved north into a rape camp, where, on all statistical evidence, she didn't survive. I trace the lines of her movement with my finger to this final pin. Even had she lived, there is no way of telling where she would have gone from here, or how, or into what new situation.

Where can this possibly take my sister? How does this advance her at all? It will only add to her grief. My breath fogs. I look over at the bowl on the mantelpiece, below it the fireplace. There's wood out the back. I could light a fire.

I turn off my headlamp and rest it in the pencil trench. But I need my map. In the dark I circle the room. I move clockwise around the draftboard, pulling my thoughts in from their tangents. I shut my eyes. The faint fall of the streetlight on my eyelids guides me, and the sound of the tram two blocks away. My boots slip on the floorboards in their curved motion, catching in the rough edges of the gaps which propel me forward. It is all predictable, I think. Either I give this map to my sister, hurt her and get my own map back. Or I burn it and keep us both here, in suspension.

I walk faster in the dark of my closed eyes, feeling the blood flow into my left side like a tide, the centrifugal force pumping the veins of my hand. I walk faster until I feel the floor shifting, unpredictable in my growing dizziness. I want to fly out of myself, be flung clear of this responsibility, all this grief which sucks me inwards, towards the map. I think I can hear the voices of the women at home, in the house of rooms, I think I can hear them speaking in whispers without faces or location as I turn, I see nothing but hear their consonants plosive on the tongue and lips in a language I now use only with my sister.

I remember my sister saying she found them in the dark when she was no longer looking, then she laughed and said no, of course she met them in all the usual places, at work, in classes, on trains and buses. They were invisible in plain sight, she said, they spoke frankly to me in their codes. They weren't even waiting to be found.

I slip and stumble but keep my eyes closed. I stop with my feet apart for balance, the angle of my feet to shins shifting, making no sense to my inner ear. I will not make any sudden adjustments, though, I will not try to catch myself in one direction or the other. It's an exercise in patience, in sangfroid. We played it as children, spinning each other by the shoulders, blindfolded. You tolerate the chaos of your pitching senses, you discipline your panic with reason, you keep your eyes closed, your feet apart, you take a deep breath and point: I know the window's there because of the way the light falls. I know you're there because you make a shadow. My sister once tricked me with a hand-held lamp: I pushed the blindfold onto my forehead and blinked. See how you can be so sure, she said, and so absolutely wrong?

But I know where I am. I know every curve of the floor-boards beneath my feet, I know the lie of the landscape that is my house better than anyone. I can never be lost, I think. I should never even be surprised. I am at the base of the draft-board, due north, the first line of my earlier measurements. I stretch out my left hand towards what I am sure is the window, waiting for the brush of the blinds on the backs of my fingers. Nothing. I open my eyes.

There is a sudden menace to the walls, the furniture, the misdirected shadows, like waking up in a strange place. I'm near the back wall, looking straight at my sister's corner. This is not the problem. The problem is that I'm facing anti-clockwise; I'm facing the wrong way.

The floor tips one way then the other. I must have turned around, somehow, at some point, I just can't remember how or when. I look right and see the back wall close to me; I put my hands to it but it slips backwards beneath my palms, the floor angles up towards me and I step forward into my sister's corner which should be the opposite one, because everything is the wrong way round. I know that I have made myself dizzy but that doesn't explain the discord of the place, the way it has flipped into its own opposite and now struggles against itself, all rhythm and balance lost.

With my hands to the plaster I turn myself around, my weight falling into the junction of the two walls. I try to relax, I try contracting and releasing my muscles, but my clothes are too tight, too warm, they clutch at my wrists and neck. My back pressed into the corner I am propped upright from two sides, my palms pressed right and left into the perpendicular walls as I wait for the passing of time to restore my house to its proper order. I watch the seconds crawl over the surfaces, wiping the threat from the floor. And it is only then, as a sense of famil-iarity returns to the arrangement of things, that I notice, in front of the draftboard, where I should have been, my sister.

She has my headlamp on, aimed at the map. I watch as her hands stretch forward to unfurl, one by one, the flags marking the positions of her lover, and the child. It's too late to stop her, to stop this unravelling she is doing, this funnelling into truth. I see her torso seize up under the pressure of it, I see her try to take air into her contracting lungs and I can't feel the

163

oxygen in my own system, I have stopped breathing in her desperation. I watch her fingernails go pale where they hold the flags. I manage to surface with a sudden spasm in my chest releasing and creating a vacuum so that the air suctions in and she looks up, gasping.

It's too late to stop her but I step forward on the floorboards which slip like driftwood under my feet. I can't stop wanting to stop her. There is no need, I feel, it could all stay scrolled up in my mind, there is no need to unroll it all like this. I reach over the height of the draftboard to grab her hands but she squirms out of my grip, she will not be held until she has finished reading them all, until she has the last little flag unfurled between her finger and thumb.

Then she grabs me as if to hurt me or drown me, and I try to pull away but she has me tight and climbs my arms to my shoulders as I push against hers, the tops of our heads close together. She shakes me and when I stop pushing I realise it's just her body trembling, my head against hers and the light below us. She doesn't make a sound but when she weeps it patters down on the map like rain.

Chapter 31

When I wake up the house is heavy, the density of the walls and doors pulling it earthward. It has been raining through the night, softening the soil to the sinking weight of the structure. I am in my own bed but nothing is mine. I have no way of knowing this place slumping in on me, nor the place which lies beneath it, nor the place that I have come from. My sister has descended and taken all the maps.

A car swishes by outside. I hold on to the bedpost to stop myself slipping into sleep, but dip down anyway, then wake suddenly as my grip relaxes and my hand bangs against the bedside table. I roll over and back into sleep, dreaming of pain in my hand. The rain on the roof like white noise.

When I wake up I know that my sister will always hate me. If it weren't for me this couldn't have happened. If it wasn't for the way I have adopted and mastered the processes that allowed it to be done, that could allow it to be done again.

The sheets are damp and clingy in the humid air. I kick them into a crumple at the foot of the bed. She will always see me as one of them. Able to prioritise form over content, process over result, able to miss the big picture for the detail. All these clichés which I am in her eyes. I haul my legs over the side of the bed. I am the walking weapon. Look at where I have brought her.

My knee aches with the rain. I limp through the house looking for a sign, a way forward, something that will indicate the path I should take from here. The dull light blurs the boundaries between objects, the lighter colours of the place indistinguishable from one another. I can only just make out that on the draftboard, scrolled in the pencil trench, is a map.

My map. My sister has brought it up in the night.

The paper rasps against my dry palms as I unroll it, its contours uncurling like tendrils. I put my face close to the surface and look westwards over the landscape of lines. My cheek cools against the paper. When I breathe in I notice that the smell of earth and paint from the basement has woven into the fibres. I look over the cliff of the mapped draftboard, the plain between the centre of the room and its western wall. Near the south-western corner, the intricate, difficult expression of the doorframe. And beyond that, the cubist rectangles of the kitchen appliances. My home.

I listen to the rain on the roof as it slows, then stops. The sun breaks through patches in the clouds. I keep my head low to the map, and watch the shadows sweep over the paper. My map, in all its constancy. While out here the weather flutters between states.

I close my eyes, release the grip of my right hand where it holds down the map and run my fingertips across its surface. I move inwards, the western edge of the map rolling itself back in over my knuckles. Each contour under my fingers is slightly indented, and can be read like Braille. I pass over the surreal, undercut contours of the mantelpiece. The wide gaps between lines as I cross the slow landscape of the floor. Then I stop.

There is something new.

A slight irregularity of texture where there shouldn't be. I open my eyes, my middle finger marking the spot. With my left hand I pull my goggles from underneath the draftboard and hold them over my eyes, pushing back the curling paper with my left elbow. I tilt my finger to one side. There is still the sound of thunder somewhere, but the glare of the morning sun is shining on the paper. I can see a tiny hole in the map, between contours, on the plain west of the mantelpiece. I lift my goggles and look over at the corresponding place on the floor. Nothing.

I push the curled edge back outwards and lift the map off the draftboard. My shadow covers the bulk of it, nothing unusual is visible. I stretch the paper taut, my arms as wide as they can go, and swing it around to the window.

Stars. The sun streams through pinpricks in the map, shining like stars. But patterned regularly, in a loose grid. They cover me in points of light, swarming over my body, glancing into my eyes with each waver of my arm or turn of my head. The nail hole at the Point of Beginning channels a broader stream, which punctures the centre of my chest.

Then the light fades in a sweep of cloud and the holes disappear. The contour lines take precedence again, and my map is returned to me, familiar. I swing it back around and smooth it into place on the draftboard, as if I could hold it in this state, unperforated or at least appearing so. A sudden clap of thunder cracks through the joints of the house. With a blast of wind the rain starts again, blowing against the window pane behind me.

I need to go in. I need to get away from all this and into the map itself; examine the holes up close, divine from magnification what could have caused them to appear. I straighten my back and grip the draftboard, waiting be taken in. I feel vulnerable, as if I were trapped outside somewhere dangerous, as if I were about to be discovered. But I can't get in. I read the lines like an amateur, skirting the surface of their symbolic value, unable to break through. I try to relax, shift the focus of my eyes in and out, sliding through all the possibilities of scale, trying to find the right one, the one that takes me in.

The rain slows again. Water from the overflowing gutter splatters into the garden bed beneath the window. I hear my sister stir below, the rustle of her sleeping bag as she extracts herself. The clink of a glass against the metal of the tap as she fills it. I don't take my eyes from the map. I fear I've lost it, the thing which opens it up to me, the key. I hear my sister gulp down the water, the syncopation of her breathing to her swallowing. A pause. My own breathing between the drips of water from the eaves.

Then the smash of shattering glass. The sound flings my gaze from the map and up into the empty room. I stand still, the walls around me blurring with reflected water. Then silence. I drop to my knees and look between the floorboards. I see the Global Map laid over my sister's table, held down by paint tubes either side. A single shard of broken glass still swivelling over the paper, until it is stopped soundlessly, by a pin.

I crawl over the floor to the corner above my sister, look through and see her shoulders as her hair falls away from her bent head, the long arc of the back of her neck. I put my palm to the boards above her. As if it would calm her. As if she would take comfort from me now. Where else would she have hidden the map, I suddenly realise, in a place as bare and exposed as that? Where else but pinned to the wall, underneath her own layer of paper?

168

The swaying of the tram sets us all rocking backwards and forwards as if praying, or insane. I hold on to my legs and let the movement bring a rhythm back to my mind. The problem, as usual, is how not to panic. There is a way to reason through this. I have never been completely blocked. It's true that this time the paper itself is irrevocably damaged. But I cannot start again, too much has gone into it. I will need to find another solution. I will need to maintain focus, think about the end point, remember why I started.

At work something is going on. There are quiet conversations in the lift but I can't catch what is being said. As I pass through the open-plan area on the way to my office I notice people huddling in groups, whispering, or just standing by their desks. They are watching the mathematician's office door as two men come out carrying the central processing unit of her computer. I wait for them to pass, then go into the office where the mathematician is alone, standing behind her desk, arms folded, lips pursed. When her eyes meet mine it's the first time I've seen her look angry. She says, —What did you do?

I just need to remember why I started and have faith that it can still be done. I will need another instrument, and a certain effort of will. This is about making the map that I need. I will have to accept the carnage of its execution.

Chapter 32

The house is lit up when I arrive home. It always is. As if it were not dissimulating, as if it were showing itself fully to the world, as if it had not been concealing things from me all this time. I was thinking about it today, at work, while they questioned me. About how it has come to this. The inconsistencies of my measurements, the changeability of the structure, the hidden rooms. How all this time I thought the problem was my failure of process, how all this time I assumed that the lie, as a result of this failure, lay in the map.

I force the front door which has swelled again with the rain and slam it closed from the inside. I go through the house, flicking off the lights. I have it all worked out. I thought about it, sitting there opposite them, while they stared at me: the Institute director, the Global Map manager, and the HR rep brought in to observe. I let their questions run over me like water and thought about what I had to do next. And why.

I wrote the steps on a Post-it so that I wouldn't later get sidetracked. They had watched me write in silence, which is an old trick. They had said everything they could and hoped I would talk out of nervousness alone.

But I am used to silence.

I pull the Post-it from my pocket now, in the darkness in front of the draftboard. Slide my headlamp over my forehead and turn it on, lighting up the yellow square of paper. It says,

1. Bring to centre

2. Structure ⟺ representation

3. Not weakened, strengthened

4. Unravel as necessary

I completed the first step at the Institute, of course, which is what they were asking about. They kept the mathematician away from me, or me from her, as if we might collude in a story, as if we might possibly be involved in the same narrative which we would benefit from getting straight. But she had nothing to do with it.

I pick up my ruler, clip on my goggles and take the new measurements at the draftboard. The diameters of the holes, their distances and orientations from one another and from the various structures marked on the map. I have to be careful, because I slide in easily tonight. There is very little holding us apart now, the map house and me, the map house and the house itself. I keep one hand held to the paper as I work, bracing myself against the draftboard, to stop the slide.

It would be dangerous to go in, with the map in this state. That's something else that occurred to me today, as the police were taking statements. I had to wait in a meeting room, where the HR rep brought me a glass of water. In her nervousness she knocked it over. The water ran through the gap between two tables, leaving no trace on the lacquered surface. That's what it would be like, I realised, with the holes, if you went into the map. You could fall out of representation and into reality or the other way round. You could disappear.

I'm fixing that now. Soon there will be no qualitative difference between the two, only one of scale. I started the first stage of the process last night, at the larger end. One to one million. I knew it could all be unified, with the necessary courage. I did only what had to be done, for the sake of safety and consistency and stability. My sister would understand.

I sense her moving below my feet.

I wouldn't have done it if it hadn't been for her. I wouldn't have been in that position, in the mathematician's office, printing out copies of the landscape which is now causing her so much pain. I wouldn't have done it if she hadn't needed this so much, or if the mathematician had returned, as I expected her to, and kept my actions within the borders of my intentions. If it hadn't become so late. But as I left her office to collect the printing I found the place empty, dark, no one left but the night cleaner hauling his trolley into the lift.

I wouldn't have thought of it, but that the opportunity was there.

It's not that I don't understand their anger. But they're not aware of the bigger picture; they don't see how what I did was essential to a larger project. I didn't try to explain. It would have sounded an inadequate justification for my actions. When the police came I just retreated inwards, closing all the doors of my mind, between me and them, between the present and the past, until I forgot what had happened, until I forgot that there was anything to say. The hum of the fluorescent light far above me. Two point five metres from my eyes I thought, two point six perhaps, depending on if I sat up straight or stayed slumped back in the chair.

The security guard in the doorway again. They took my swipe card and told me to leave the building. Apparently they can press charges, which surprised me: I didn't think it was that bad. It's just a map, after all.

I went straight to the hardware store. All my forking paths threading back to one.

Even at high magnification the holes seem perfectly round. I find it pleasurable to measure their diameters in several orientations and have my vernier callipers repeatedly lining up, to within one-fiftieth of a millimetre, on the same figures. I breathe through my mouth. There is a beauty to them, the way they are so tiny yet so absolute in their piercing. It feels strange, to start so small, to start from this end of things and move outwards rather than in. I take care because the potential for error is greater this way round. Or rather, any error made will be magnified, in projection.

When I have finished measuring I lift my goggles and stare at the figures on my notepad until they come back into focus. I can hear my sister tapping at something in the basement below. The sound seems far away and does not disturb me. I make the calculations by hand, with pen and paper. It demands intense concentration, and is difficult at first. But after an hour the relationship of numbers has settled into my mind like instinct. It is good preparation for what I am about to do.

I put down my pen and let my hand run over the map. The straining of its lines, the effort it has undertaken to make sense of its surroundings. The damage it has had to endure. The source of all my difficulties is not in there, but out here.

When I turn on the overhead light the room expands around me in all directions. The transfer outwards is a pleasant sensation. After the intensity of micromillimetres, working with centimetres feels almost reckless. I move around the room in great strides, marking up the floorboards with chalk, the tape measure stiff in my hand. It's hard to maintain focus and not start laughing, with all the numbers inside me like bubbles.

I had chosen the heaviest drill the hardware store stocked. My hands look small as I prise it now from its packaging on the marked-up floor; the sinews in my arm straining as I take its weight. The drill bits are lined up in their polystyrene niches. I run my fingers across them like a keyboard, imagining the different pitches they will hit when turned. I measure their diameters and select the one which, scaled-up, is appropriate to the width of a pinprick. Insert it, check everything, plug the machine into an extension cord running from the kitchen.

I am unused to the force and recoil the first time I turn it on.

It will do the job. If the representation escapes the structure, then the structure must be brought into line. I don't know why I didn't see it before. The map is not a lie, the house is.

Chapter 33

The house is lit up as I expand outwards in ever increasing circles with the drill ringing. I have turned out the lights again and now the glow from the basement pierces the structure not only through the gaps between the floorboards but also through the holes I have created.

The machine slides through my books and folders like butter and leaves them smouldering. I do the smaller objects separately over the kitchen sink, then return them to their proper place, align them one on top of the other until they catch the light from the basement below which streams up through them all like the path of a bullet.

I look up. The ceiling is dotted in perfect projection of what I'd seen this morning, when the light from the window shone through the map. The agreement isn't complete, but it is getting there. Next I pace across the room, looking at the holes in the floor. The light from below stops me seeing through to the basement.

There's a layer missing. I pull the Post-it from my pocket. Stage three: Not weakened, strengthened. For that I need to go down.

The handle of the cupboard turns soundlessly under my hand, the door swings open without effort, as if force were no longer required. The stairs are lit up from below, and I go down clear-headed and sure-footed. The basement is frosted with sawdust from my drilling; the open cupboard door now creates a draft which suctions air from above and whirls the dust in a slow spiral on the tiled floor.

My sister is in the centre of the room, at her table, hammering broken glass into the Global Map of our country. I watch as she taps the sharpest splinters through the paper to pin them to the wood below. And then takes rougher fragments and smashes down with all her force so that the shards are embedded into the paper itself, leaving it gleaming in the light.

I walk towards her in the dust until I am at the vortex of its circling, the point of stillness, close to the table where my sister is working. I watch her painting with her fingers in the space between the shards and the flags, across the wooded areas and fields of our country. I watch her swirl the paint up off the paper in spirals where there are cities. I stand opposite her watching her hands move as if they were my own. I feel the sting where she has cut her fingertips on the glass and smears blood in places along the roads.

I would slide in but for the scratching sound I can hear. I would slide into the country she is creating of our home, I would slide along the roads with her fingers and into the villages, I would see again the town squares, the boarded-up windows, the teenage soldiers kicking in the doors. The scratching sound keeps me here, and it is the reason I have come down.

It comes from under her table. I crouch down and see, through the shadows, the rolled-up draft I made of the basement. It rocks on the swell of the floor in perpetual motion, its edge scraping at the tiles. I reach forward through the turning dust and grasp it. When I straighten up my sister is still working, head down, as if I were not even there. The dust tumbling like water over my shoes.

She leans forward across the paper towards me. Her head is bent and close to mine. She is applying paint with a matchstick to a point beside a road, a farmed area not far from a village. She works the paint into the same point over and over until the paper is almost worn through. Her hair is tied back off her face. I see her shut her eyes. She has my earplugs in.

33.5

The sister goes soundlessly through the motions of painting and wonders how to move on. She has taken the map to the various agencies and non-government organisations, hoping the new coordinates would open the whole thing up. The officials were sympathetic, understanding that this new data must occasion a freefall of probability, that her chances of seeing her lover and the child again were now approaching zero. Approaching, though, not arriving. The sister would be informed, they said, if any new information on her loved ones became available.

She tries painting with her eyes shut. Drops the matchstick she has been working with and tries to sniff out the colours from their tubes, feel their texture between finger and thumb, the density of black, the acrid odour of red, the slipperiness particular to indigo. She tries to mix them to exactly the right viscosity between her fingers, brush or smear them onto the paper with a certain pressure, a certain sound. She finds white by its thinness in the tin and wants to put it to her lips, feel it stain her teeth and throat, drink it down and fill her with a blankness appropriate to the void. She would speak air, speak the absence of colour and words, her tongue coated with loss. It would be damaging to hear.

But where would that get her? She puts the tin down and opens her eyes.

33.75

The map is lit up under my headlamp as I slide the draft of the basement underneath it on the draftboard. I align them both over the Point of Beginning, drive a new nail through the hole. They curl upwards together from having been rolled, and I press them down at the sides with the sliding rulers.

I put on my goggles and headlamp to look closer. The contours of the basement are now visible through each of the pinpricks in the original map. This is appropriate, and I could not have divined, through reason or skill, a better solution. My map, shot through with absence, perforated by that which it had failed to represent. More accurate as a result, and more expressive of the complexity of its referent. Not weakened, but strengthened.

They wouldn't understand this idea, at the Institute. You need to have gone through a process, you need to have been cartographically challenged by a multi-levelled landscape before a solution like this one can come to be seen as viable. They've never had to deal with any of that; they've only ever mapped solid ground. That became obvious to me as I went through the files on the mathematician's computer. It was clear from the pedestrian way they were constructing the Global Map.

I pull the Post-it from my pocket and shine the headlamp on it. Three of the four stages are complete. But I need to work quickly, before the first is undone at the Institute. They will be staying up all night like me. They will be trying to change it back. But they won't know where to start. I'm surprised the mathematician hasn't guessed.

33.875

The sister looks at her painting on the map of her country and thinks that she is going too hard. She tries lightness of touch, as if it will help, she aims to skirt the depths but not get sucked down. She waters down her paints and builds colour in layers, repeating form with minor alterations, adding shade and detail systematically, almost cartographically, as if complexity could be constructed out of persistence alone.

Chapter 34

The house is lit up behind me as I squint through the peephole of the front door, into the darkness outside. An internal pressure pushes against my skin and organs. I feel that I could explode, that I could do it all, that it all has to be done at once. In all directions, on all scales. I have started on the house before finishing the map, I will come back to the map before finishing the house. But it is all coming together. This map of how hard it is to make a map. This map of the effort itself.

I don't have long. A small window of time as my colleagues at the Institute try to come to terms with the sudden shift they now see in their Global Map. They will need to run tests to determine what has happened, and why, and where it has taken them. And only then, should they get that far, can they begin recalibrating the data sets, cross-checking the figures, ensuring that no inconsistencies remain. The tedious task of returning to normal.

It will take at least several days, possibly weeks, but that's their problem for wanting to change it back. The choice was always arbitrary, and there is no qualitative difference between one arbitrarily chosen reference point and another. Every map needs a point of beginning, the fixed point in the landscape around which the grid is centred, from which the measurements are theoretically taken. Something which will endure, something which will be there through all but the most unpredictable, catastrophic events. Why they chose something

182

as fragile as a flagpole on a parliament is beyond me. It's much safer here, aligned with my own Point of Beginning. Inconspicuous, apolitical and guarded by someone with a knowledge of maps.

My action was not selfish, it has simply served me by chance. It's true it has allowed me to bring it all together. My map, and the Global Map for this country, both circling around the same point, differing only in scale. Adding power to them both.

But it won't last, I remind myself. They are changing it back right now, as I stand here staring at the street. I understand that I can't keep everything, but I want to make some progress while I have the data on my side. It's a complex project for so little time. Speed will not help me now. I need some miracle of physics, some unfolding of the continuum, some sudden solution from an unforeseen direction. It's likely that I won't succeed. But this is no longer the point.

I just need to know when I'm as close as I'm ever going to get.

34.5

The sister chases her fingers across the paper, she climbs and riffs, circling the flags, staying just ahead of herself through the glass and blood. She scrapes her fingernails down through a spectrum of scaled colour, mounts again, sweeps the paint in a long curve with a knuckle, then flaps the flat of her hand against a blob of paint in a splatter of a stop. She steps back, tilts her head and regains her breath. Satisfied by the process but disappointed with the result.

34.75

Through the distorted glass of the peephole I think I see a police car go by. I curl my fingers to my palms and hold on. They are waiting for me to lose it. But I know where I am and what to do next. I turn my back to the door and face down the planes of the corridor.

These irregular constricting walls. These flimsy constructions which attempt to trick me into believing they mean something, as if they must, for the sake of methodological consistency, be accounted for. They simply slice up the space, break it into compartments. Not only divisive, but damaging to understanding. They conceal, and betray. Think of the basement.

Which brings me to stage four. Unravel as necessary.

34.875

The sister looks at the Global Map of her country, or rather at her painting of it, over it. The form is disappearing under the weight of her working of it. The flags tilt in the swamp of texture she has swirled around them.

Under the paint, under the contours, is her country, a country that no longer exists. The sister takes the pin marking the place where her lover was last held and turns it in increasing circles, widening the hole beneath it. She needs something else here, something that will draw the eye, suck everything in, pull perspective down into a whirlpool of absence. A connection between the world and what it is trying to forget.

She looks up.

Chapter 35

The house is lit up all through the night as I think of the basement and search for other rooms I might have missed. I examine the surfaces of all the doors and walls, looking for cracks or inconsistencies, I open the drawers in the kitchen and compare their lengths to the bench top above, I check the backs of all the cupboards, rapping my knuckles over the surfaces till they bleed.

It will all need to come undone.

I start gently, with inconspicuous tools. I untwist screws with a teaspoon, pluck at nails with tweezers, tug at the joints with my bare hands. But it takes too much time, and leaves the larger structures intact. It is not enough.

I will need an axe, a sledge-hammer and a circular saw.

35.5

The sister hears her twin slam the front door. She goes up the basement stairs and sees that the kitchen cupboards have been dismantled. Objects removed from drawers and shelves are lined up on the map room floor in the morning light. Among them a drill and a ball of string.

The sister lies with her head under the draftboard looking up. The nail marking the Point of Beginning breaks through the wood at an angle. She reaches up and ties one end of the string to its tip. She lets the ball unravel to a point just above the floor and ties it so that it swings from the Point of Beginning like a pendulum. When it stops she marks the place on the floor below it centre, takes up the electric drill lying nearby and makes a hole. She unties the ball of string, slides her finger inside and hooks out the other end, then threads it through the hole.

Back down in the basement she has only to lean on the table and reach up. She tugs the string through the hole, feels it unravel as the ball jumps and diminishes on the floorboards above. The string ripples through her hands into a tangle on her table, until finally it tightens in her grip; a single line from her fingers to the underside of the draftboard above. She pulls her fingers down its length to the point just above the table, fastens a wad of putty as a weight and lets it swing to the perpendicular. The correspondence of the Point of Beginning on this, lower, map. She pulls the table so that the putty hovers over the pin made into a flag to mark the position of where her lover was last held. Then she ties the string to the pin, presses it deep into the plywood of the table below and cuts away the excess.

She puts the CD player on high and adjusts the bassline until it vibrates the string.

Chapter 36

When I arrive home the house is pulsing with music which pushes out through all the spaces in the structure. It slips me sideways from the front path and into the overgrown garden. I lean backwards into the fence railings, holding the hardware store box to my chest, among the flowers which have blasted open, strangled by weeds.

I am six point four metres from the map room window. The blinds are open as I left them, the morning sun illuminating the room beyond, the air bruised by the sound. I think I see my sister moving in and out of the frame. I haul myself upright and push forward until I can rest the box on the window sill, jammed against the glass by my body. I lean over it and cup my hands around my eyes to look in properly. She is gone. But the order of things has changed.

I pull the box back to my chest, take its full weight and push forward, the music pushing back, until I reach the front door. I slide the key into the lock, hear the deadlock clunk. Drag the box from the front porch into the corridor, put my weight behind it and shove it into the map room. From my hands and knees I see what my sister has done. The drill has been moved. The ball of string has disappeared, and there is a single thread running taut from the bottom of the Point of Beginning, down into her basement.

This doesn't bother me. It seems right. I kick the front door shut.

Now that I am inside the music is no longer pushing me but pulling. It tugs me to my feet and into the map room where I notice it is shaking those parts of the structure which must come down. I put my finger tips to an inner wall and follow the vibrations to their epicentre; the middle of the back wall. It shudders at my touch.

The music builds in a slow movement, the full orchestral force of it thudding through the beams. I don't know why it has taken me so long to come to this point. I don't know why it has had to be so hard and demanded so much effort from me. But the process has its own running in it now. It courses through the lower part of the structure and up into the bones of my feet and legs. It swells up in me like a crescendo.

I pull the axe from the hardware store box and destroy the back wall first. There is a joy and a tragedy to both the action and the result. The inside of the flayed walls is breathtaking. There are wires of all colours, there are mysterious grey tubes running like veins from corner to corner, piping the house like an organ. I pull out all its stops. The plasterboard breaks off in my hands and showers me with dust. The music of the house calls out in every direction; it has melodies running over each other like turbulence. I leave the web of wires intact so they can continue to pump the electricity which lights it. I reach between them and slap at the cool, undisturbed bricks, the same bricks that I have touched from the backyard. As inside, so out.

36.5

Over the thump of the music the sister listens to her twin axing the walls. She wonders if this new focus on the physical structure means her twin has given up on representation. The thought makes her take to her painting with renewed vigour. Each swing of her twin's axe sends waves reverberating down the string into the paper.

As the sister paints through the ripples she becomes aware of the growing force of the blows and hopes her twin remembers that she is here. She has accepted relegation to this invisible space for the sake of her twin, but she did not intend to completely disappear. She looks up at what is keeping a lid on her, at what to her sister is merely a starting point, a surface on which to move. She wonders if she has given herself enough with this space, if she isn't letting herself be compartmentalised and forgotten. What is she settling for now?

At the top of the stairs she finds she has locked herself in. She searches between the boxes on the cupboard floor for the hairpin she uses and finds only dust. She bangs on the inside of the door but cannot be heard over the music. By the time she turns it off and comes back up the stairs, the house is quiet.

Chapter 37

The house is lit up from where I stand on the footpath in the dark. Cracks zigzag between the bricks seeping light from the interior now that the inner walls are gone. The house is bleeding light, its windows glassy with pain.

I will have nothing concealed. I will not be a foreigner in my own home, ignorant of what lies within a wall, unable to sense the doorways in the dark, unable to predict if, or when, I am going to fall. I will possess it with its own processes, and I will do this even if I have to destroy everything I have and have made. Or else I will be forever on the outside. My sister thinks the only alternative is to want something different as if the wanting of something alone could bring it into existence. But this is a better idea.

I kneel at the front door and whisper into the keyhole. I say, —I will know all of you, I will measure your every dimension, I will trace your every line. I say, —You will not elude me, I will undo you from the inside. You will feel it like waves running across your floorboards, you will feel it like water rising through your walls, you will feel it like a sudden disorientation, you will wonder what happened to your foundations.

37.5

The sister stands in the dark in front of her table holding on to the string. The silence above makes her feel trapped. She listens for the return of her twin, not liking not knowing where she is. She follows the line of the string upwards to the point of light which streams through the hole in the floor above. It feels tenuous in her hand. She climbs on to the table, sliding in the wet paint. She curls herself like putty around the string.

37.75

The house darkens as I pad through the rooms, flicking off the lights. I go back to the source. At the draftboard I squeeze on the headlamp and the map lights up like eyes opening. I am locked in its gaze. I can barely believe that I have done this, that I have come this far, that I have brought all these lines and shapes out of nothing but the space around me. I have brought this into existence with persistence alone and now it is bigger than me, it is pulling at me, it wants to break its borders and expand outwards. I have to give it its full scope. It is not for me to say where it ends.

The paper was just the start. I will extend my representation outwards in all directions, like an explosion. The map will be infinite in scope because it will have no borders. It will be infinite in detail for the same reason. Why didn't I see this before? Why couldn't I see beyond the limits I had placed on myself as I clipped the paper to the draftboard, why didn't I notice that its edges were frayed?

37.875

The string is tugging at the sister as she sleeps, and she finds herself following it back into the past, her twin's city, through doors and streets. It frays on the brick corners of buildings, it climbs over roofs and tangles on the descent. She follows it, constantly fearing she will lose it, constantly fearing it is already gone. It slithers through her fingers burning. She twists it around her thumb to hook it in, feels the pressure of built-up blood, she watches the pink of her flesh turn blue, but she's got it now, she realises this may be what it takes, she feels it wire-cut her skin and wonders if a finger wouldn't be a more practical sacrifice, she wonders in that case which one.

Chapter 38

The house is lit up under my fingers as I tear through it flicking switches, pressing buttons, illuminating every invention designed to do so. I set it humming with electricity from all its bulbs and in the bathroom run my ruler over the xylophone tiles. I was not wrong about the composition of this place but I was too limited in my choice of instruments. It needs an orchestra. I take to the tiles with a crowbar, syncopating my rhythm to the strum of the washing machine. In the kitchen the kettle sings.

I miss the delicacy of my micro measurements but the big picture must be dealt with first. How else can anything small be true? I miss my precision instruments as I axe the beams themselves, lending an instability to the structure that more accurately reflects the outside world but creates a mild thread of panic that I drag with me through the rooms, tangling, from time to time, around my ankles and causing me to trip.

I always recover.

I cover the draftboard with a sheet, put what I need in a backpack, stack my furniture under the manhole and climb into the ceiling. I straddle the rafters in the dark, take the sledge-hammer from the backpack and bash at the plaster till it rains down on the rooms below. The light shines up through the holes and I see the floor of the map room far away. I drop my legs over the side, grip the ceiling beam with both hands and hang my body into the space. When I let go the floor hits me hard with an equal and opposite force, as if it were a solid thing, as if it were not keeping the basement from me. As if it were as low as I could go.

38.5

The sister knows her lover is beside her, as she dreams her nightmares, knows it with every sense but sight. She can smell her lover's hair, feel the heat of her body, taste the wetness of her breath as she wrapped them both in a blanket, at an outdoor cinema she remembers from a trip to see her twin in the city. She sees her lover in profile laughing at the screen, before the jokes, before anyone else, as if she could feel them coming. The sister laughing with her lover, and so missing the joke. Their faces flickering with light. Then she is woken by the sound of her twin falling to the floor above her; she opens her eyes, and is alone.

When the wheel of the circular saw breaks through the boards she doesn't move, but stays curled around the string. Let it all come crashing down, she thinks.

38.75

I slice up the floorboards with calculation, so that they are severed in key places but do not fall until I am ready. I explain my methodology to my sister through the gaps. —Stay where you are, I tell her, and you will be perfectly safe.

I will have all pathways leading to the draftboard and radiating from it. The boards fall away to create suspended walkways to the other rooms, the windows and doors. It means cutting triangles; it is a beautifully simple trigonometry of exposure. Why have I been content with mapping only what already exists, with trying to know instead of contributing to knowledge, with interpretation rather than creation?

My sister doesn't answer. In the doorway between the corridor and the map room I balance on the creaking beams and take the Post-it note from my pocket. Unravel as necessary. I am nearly there.

38.875

The sister looks up from her table at the wheel of beams and boards above her, radiating out from the square of floor which is all that otherwise remains, holding up the draftboard. The square that has protected her and her table and her painting. Through the triangles of empty space she sees the exposed rafters of the ceiling high above, her twin climbing among them, measuring. The sister stands up on the table and looks around her at the shattered floorboards on the broken tiles of the basement, where they have fallen.

She thinks now that things have been bad for too long. She wonders if it is not a matter of perception and if she has not therefore slipped into some negative, some antiworld where everything will always look wrong, as if she were trapped under the glass of her own eyes, as if she had lost the knack to living without fear, the instinct for optimism, the bone-deep blessing of hope. She decides it is time to reverse the process. She wants to climb now, she wants to work her way back.

Chapter 39

When I wake up the house is dark. It is the middle of the night and I am sure my sister's lover is alive. I can hear her scrambling over the roof tiles, trying to draw attention to herself, to my sister, to me. Trying to wake us up.

Wide awake I listen to the house. Nothing. Only my bedside clock chinking the silence.

I need my sister. She has climbed out of the basement and is sleeping under the draftboard. I edge across the beams to her and shake her awake.

—Did you hear her? I ask.

My sister just looks at me through half-closed eyes. —I hear her all the time, she says.

There is a pain somewhere in the house like a nerve exposed to the air. I feel it in my teeth and scalp. It rings in the darkness at a pitch almost too high to hear. The source is somewhere small, in a tiny part of something, concealed, or else hidden among the layers of something ordinary.

While my sister sleeps I rip the lining out of my clothes and bags, pull the soles from my shoes. I tear through all these fabrications, break everything into its component parts: the alarm clock, my laptop, the fridge. I lay out the pieces in rows along the exposed crossbeams of the map room floor. The microchips are signalling and I attempt interception. I expect nothing. Like a true scientist, I impose no interpretation on the results before me. I will have no more unquestioned assumptions. I will not be gutted, I will do the gutting. I will pull the bones from my house, I will fillet it, splay it open, I will read, in its entrails, everything I need to learn.

39.5

When the sister wakes up the house is dark and huge, the shattered ceiling a sky away and the beams of the flayed walls stretching to the horizons. She is in an ocean of architecture, everything else submerged, her home, her mother, her lover, all below the leagues and leagues of it, sunk in the pressured depths and leaving the sister here, floating above it all on a raft. She grasps the sides of the sawn wood and pulls her upper body over the edge. She peers down into the basement in the pre-dawn darkness and sees her twin, with her headlamp on, searching through paint jars for something she doesn't find.

39.75

The house is lit up as the sun rises and cuts the darkness into triangles on the rubble of the basement floor. I feel my sister watching me from the draftboard's platform above. As she shifts her weight the sunlight breaks through the hole she has drilled in the floorboards for the string to pass through. I see the light travel down the string to the pin she has pressed into her lowest point and I see she has done it as if to hold me there, as if to connect my mapping to all that pain. I put my ear to the string and think that this is what I can feel in the rhythm of the structure, that this is the sense of it, and the source.

39.875

The sister works directly onto the beams and doorframes. She paints faces with their mouths set, eyes pinched, until they are everywhere, haunting the house. She paints her lover's face at various points, lost among the crowds. Her twin continues unaware, noticing only the structure.

39.9375

As I move through the house I feel the ringing inside me like a thread vibrating, cutting at my organs but holding me to my sister. I am unable to unhook myself from her though it would seem a simple gesture, there would be something deceptive about the comfort and release it would provide. I move through the structure now shattered and exposed thinking this is what I need to live with after all, this is what it is when all the lies are removed. I will not block myself off from it any more, will not make containment my routine.

In the house of rooms the walls were not so much partitions as connections joining the different spaces together. There were so many of them that you were always linked to alternatives and could change as you passed through the doorways into something new. I could feel paint on my fingers warm in the summer heat with my sister showing me how to work it in the high room above the courtyard and the flies blowing in from outside. I could feel the sweat on my upper lip as I breathed and worked my hands moving colour on the canvas and it was all as real to me as language, as numbers, as my sister is now.

The new walls here will be made of string or light so that they can be parted with breath alone, with the act of speaking and the willingness to step through.

Through my goggles I can see that the map has never been completely still. There are harmonics to the lines, invisible to the naked eye, their vibrations following the act of creation, shadowing the original and lending a sense of depth to the work. I am reluctant to cut it, but so much of the detail has now become irrelevant in the face of the changing structure. I slide cardboard between the two layers, take a razor blade and begin the incisions in precise triangles on the area representing the map room floor, faithful to the measurements I have taken through the night. When I pull back the cardboard, the draft of the basement shows through the gaps. It will have to be updated, too, of course.

39.96875

The sister has heard the slam of a car door outside and edged along a crossbeam to look through the blinds. A white car is in front of the house, red government numberplates glowing in the morning light.

39.984375

The mathematician is standing in my front garden in full view of the world and, from the opposite perspective, me. She frowns at me through the window, as if I were a problem that could be solved. But she is missing data that I will not provide.

I could hear her voice, but not the words, as they interviewed her in a meeting room next to the one that I had been placed in. I could see in my mind's eye the same lacquered table but without the water running through the gaps. She looks at me now as if she is waiting for an explanation and I find myself searching for an argument that she would warm to, because I would like to convince her of something, I would like to see her fall back to her default of trust in me.

My sister says I should let her in but if she were to see the state of my house she would think there was something disproportionate about me. She would decide that I am not worth the effort or risk. I look around and wonder what I might be able to change, quickly, effortlessly, or what, rather, I might able to hide. But to what end? My sister says again that I should let her in and I say, —Why? Doesn't she have a home to go to?

Her presence cannot possibly benefit me, and contact with me cannot possibly benefit her. I reach to the cord and flick the blinds closed.

39.9921875

It's her missing of her lover that makes her want to let everyone in. It's why she makes no distinction between inside and outside, because all that desire sucks like a vacuum and she is wall-less in her wanting.

But the pressure inside me is atmospheric, buoying me, pushing me onwards. Action is the only option. I run through the house taking measurements, pulling it apart. My hands move with a speed that cannot be reasoned, I map like a pianist, my fingering leaving my thoughts behind. Everything is on track. I see well, calculate clearly, move with certainty. The house is my talent and I am born to it. I measure and expose, reveal then re-evaluate.

The mathematician knocks and knocks.

My sister will not stop following me. Sometimes she helps. She pulls with me when a part of the house resists, she throws her force behind mine with each swing of the sledge-hammer. She holds on to me as I balance on a ceiling rafter, as I reach up and hook my tape measure to the inside of a roof tile. She is taller than me and so holds the end in place as we look down and watch it unroll under its own weight to the basement floor. I didn't know my house had such depth, such height, that it was so far from apex to trough.

She is more distracted by the mathematician's knocking than I am. In the end, although we are both standing at the door, it is her hands that open it.

The mathematician stands in the doorway looking at me like she will not give up. Behind her the neighbourhood children shout to each other from their bicycles.

—I've got something for you, she says.

—What?

She unzips her bag without taking her eyes from me.

—They haven't worked it out yet, she adds.

I raise my eyebrows.

—Where you started I mean, she says. —They just know the data is not where it used to be, that the old referent isn't working any more.

—They don't know? I ask.

—No.

—Do you?

—Yes.

—Why don't you tell them?

—They'll work it out eventually.

She dips her head and takes something small from her bag. She hands over a new USB stick.

—What's this? I ask.

—It's the map as it is now. The data. With your Point of Beginning. So that it's saved, even when they change it back.

39.99609375

The sister stands behind the door as her twin talks to the mathematician. She looks through the peephole and can see the mathematician's face, side on, the way she has hooked a long piece of hair behind her ear. She watches as the mathematician purses her lips in a sign of distrust. She sees the small signals that her twin doesn't pick up, indicating resistance, or possibly vulnerability. The mathematician smiles and the lines around her eyes crinkle. She dips her head, hands something over and leaves.

The sister realises she forgot to listen to the conversation.

Chapter 40

I look at the new USB stick in my hand. I attach it to the same string as the other one, around my neck. They can swing there together, enclosing my two countries: the one I lost, and the one I made up, with me at the centre.

I go back to my draftboard and place my left index finger on the nail head at the centre of the draftboard. This is the Point of Beginning and they haven't found it yet. The Global Map of this country hovers invisible, under my finger. My own map of my house stretches out from here too. And the string my sister has tied to its underside links it to the Global Map of my home country below.

All my countries brought together, here, at this one point. My left hand tingles. And the house is lit up.